JENNIFER GIBBS

Noticed

Thank you so
much for
your
support!
♡, Jennifer
Gibbs

This book is dedicated to my parents. The ones who believed in me even more than I believed in myself.

Contents

Acknowledgement

I would like to acknowledge my husband, Mike, and my daughters, Caroline and Courtney. They have provided me with endless inspiration in my writing and in my life. My biggest hope is to make them proud.

I would like to acknowledge my profession and my students. As a school counselor, I'm given the greatest gift. With the opportunity to peek in at the future generations, I'm in awe of their resilience, creativity, and curiosity. It is a true joy to share in their stories.

Chapter One—Cassidy Maxwell

BEEP...BEEP...BEEP. AHH! Ouch! Dammit! My elbow hits my bedpost as I start swatting at my alarm clock. The pain radiates up my arm as I begin shaking my arm back and forth, and sleepily focus my eyes on the clock. The clock displays 5:30, and I hit snooze and sluggishly roll back over bleary-eyed and half asleep. I always set the clock fifteen minutes before I have to get up, so I can think about the day ahead of me. I relish those moments without the constant chatter of the other people that live in my house who incessantly invade my brain space—Mom, Dad, and Charlotte, my little sister. Every morning, the people in our house scurry around like little ants, opening drawers, searching for shoes, slamming cabinets, and making a mad dash out the door. My sister, Charlotte, starts in with the questions from the second her feet hit the floor, "Is it going to be cold today? Should I wear tights? Do we have anything to do afterschool today?" So, I lay there enjoying this moment of solitude and thinking about the historic day ahead.

One of the more monumental things in my life is happening today, April 7th. I am going to get my driver's license at the DMV this morning. Officially a driver, that's right, one step closer

1

to actual freedom. Some of my friends aren't in a rush to get their license because they enjoy being chauffeured around. Lots of them are scared and have barely practiced. Not me, I have been counting down the days and driving any chance I can get. I don't get this at all. At my school, lots of kids wake up on their birthday to a new or newish car parked in the driveway with a big, red bow stretched across the hood. This may sound cliché, and it is. In our suburban area, it is the norm to make grand gestures for your kids. I have often wondered if the display is really necessary, but who am I kidding it's not like I would complain if my parents decided to do it. No such luck, of course! My parents are both from middle-class upbringings with no-frills parents, so I am in for sharing a car with my mom, or possibly getting a used one that I will pay for with a little help from my parents. I have been saving some money from babysitting, so I am about two thousand dollars away from being able to buy the car I want, a used Volkswagen Rabbit convertible. I haven't broken this to my mom yet because she'll never approve of a convertible without some serious begging and pleading. She and my dad have even been known to have me create presentations (backed by research, mind you!) for them when I am trying to persuade them. But, first things first.

I start quizzing myself in my head for the millionth time about road signs and road rules, and all of the things I have studied in the Driver's Manual. Lying on my bed, I see my outfit laid out down to the shoes. I am wearing a solid blue shirt because I read somewhere that solids photograph better than prints, and white jeans, with silver hoop earrings, and camel-colored flats. *Should be perfect.*

As the clock seems to race to 5:45, I peel myself out of bed one leg at a time. No matter what time I wake up, it is always hard to force myself out of my cozy, queen-sized bed with flannel sheets and with my gray and cream throw pillows perched between my knees. I love to bury myself in my down comforter with my phone in hand. Typically, I lie there texting until the wee hours of the morning, usually to my best friend, Madison. I don't think there is a thought that has ever popped in our minds that we didn't eventually share with each other. During our middle school years, we would always say we were basically sisters, but truly, we are, fights and all. My bedroom has become my safe haven in the last two years. My favorite place, my hideaway, my refuge where I can escape the peering eyes of my overinvolved mother.

Just then, as if on command, Mom appears at the door. Still in her nightgown, a little bleary-eyed herself, she hovers at the door. I look over at her, and she just stands there staring at me.

"What?" I said.

"Just making sure you were awake," she explained.

This is kind of normal for us. Sometimes I just catch her staring at me. It is weird. She says it is because I have changed so much in the last few years. And, I really have. I look back at pictures of my 10-year-old self, and see a short, little girl, with squatty legs, and medium-length blonde hair falling towards my face. Since then, my legs have lengthened, my torso has stretched, and my hair now reaches well beyond my shoulders, darkening slightly over the years to a sandy blonde. Every now and then,

3

I am even taken aback when I look in the mirror and see the beginnings of a womanly figure.

"Why are you staring at me?" I grumbled.

"Oh, I'm not, I'm just zoning out for a minute. Hurry, we have got to leave on time, so we can make it to get your license and then to school in time for a faculty meeting I have to attend," she said with some urgency.

Mom and I are used to spending lots of time together. When I was younger we were known as two peas in a pod. We would run errands together, and we would do all kinds of things to make our chores more enjoyable like use funny accents, make up raps for the car ride, or pretend we were on a top-secret mission. Sometimes I really miss those times and her.

Even then, just like now, Mom would ask my advice about things and get my input before making major decisions. It may seem strange, but I have always been known for giving shockingly good advice. I remember people always describing me as 'deep' when I was younger, or say I seemed mature beyond my years. I would have endless questions about life, faith, and people. I remember things like "why didn't Santa give the poor children just as many presents as everyone else," filled my head. And, I was notorious for asking one 'what if' question after another. I was the compassionate one among my friend group. I had even earned the title of "Mom" among my friends which could sometimes be funny, but sometimes make me just want to prove them wrong, and shock them with something rebellious or dangerous. But among friends and adults alike, I was often

4

referred to as a little counselor in training. I was and still am the go-to girl for my friends for advice on boys, parent problems, and girl drama.

Come to think of it, I don't think my own Mom has ever made a major decision without getting my take on it. I remember her asking if I thought we should move out of our old neighborhood, and if she should take a job as a counselor at the high school I would eventually attend. Even then, I knew it would be weird. My major concern was that she would meddle too much in my life. No, she promised, she wouldn't dare, but not surprisingly, she was never able to stop herself. Every year, she has tweaked my school schedule to make sure I'd get the right mixture of teachers for my personality, not too harsh, but who would still push me when I needed it. She always made sure I had a friend or two in my classes because she rationalized that I spoke up more in class if I felt confident. She would call it a little fine-tuning or just small adjustments to make sure I was secure and happy. Dad would argue with her that she was protecting me too much—shielding me at every turn and stunting my growth. His concerns didn't do much if anything to deter her.

Mom finally leaves my bedroom and closes my door which snaps me back into the routine of getting ready. Walking into the bathroom, and turning on the lights, I give myself the once-over. My normally bright, blue eyes are slightly bloodshot and puffy. My skin is still tanner than normal from a recent trip to the beach, and my teeth are bright white from all of the whitening toothpaste I have been using. After getting my braces off, I have been obsessed with my smile. Jumping in the shower, I practice my smile for my driver's license picture. It can't be too big, but just a small upturned smile from the corners will be perfect.

After getting showered, straightening my hair, and putting on a little make up, I am ready to grab some breakfast and head out the door. On my way down the hall, I just can't resist peeking in on Charlotte. Her nine-year-old little body is splayed out diagonally across her queen-sized bed. I see her dark head of hair tousled in front of her freckled, pale face. Her room as always is quite the disaster with stuffed animals, dolls, and construction paper on the floor. As I look in closer, I see she has been making something with a cardboard box. This makes a big, broad grin stretch across my face. This is so Charlotte. The cardboard is a stage for her stuffed animals and her dolls. This kid is always creating—always! Charlotte is always asking Mom questions like "Can I have that cardboard box? Paper roll? Those scraps of paper you aren't using?" Each time, we all know what this means—a new Charlotte creation and a big mess. She is constantly trying out her cooking creations where she grabs whatever she can find, and begins microwaving, stirring, combining, and finally, achieving an end product that looks like something our dog, Bentley, will reject or even worse, something the Bentley has yakked up. I love that little kid, though. Charlotte is my ultimate admirer, and even though she can be annoying, she does make life more fun.

Mom is always encouraging Charlotte, and me, too, for that matter. She has always been *that* mom, telling us we were special and hoping we would believe it. She would encourage our creativity and 'spirit' as she would call it. She said she hoped we would be stronger than her and not let the questions creep in.

I remember not knowing what she was talking about it, and she said, "You know, those doubts like maybe I'm just like everyone else, or maybe I'm never going to be exceptionally good at anything, or maybe I don't have a real purpose." Mom was always questioning herself. Maybe she was going through some type of midlife crisis or something. I stare at Charlotte one more time, and close her door quietly.

I enter Mom and Dad's room to tell them I am ready. Dad is already up and combing his hair. He seriously takes all of ten minutes to get ready for work. So, this is his routine to a T, he showers, get dressed in the usual 'uniform' of dress pants and golf shirt, combs his thick head of dark hair, and then stares at us like we are the slowest people on the planet. My dad is the definition of a morning person. He is energized from the moment he wakes up, always trying to start up a conversation with us when we are in a rush. Somehow he is able to ramble on without a break, or by adding in an 'um..' timed ever so perfectly, so you can't wiggle in even one word. These conversations are not what I would call a real conversation, but more of a list of things we really need to get done. It is mostly directed at Mom, and usually begins as a reminder that he had checked the credit card bill and it was already shaping up to be a banner month, and not in a good way.

"Dad, do you remember what today is?" I ask.

"Hmm... let me think, is it 'National Hug Your Dad Day'?" he jokes.

"Very funny. How about your 'Worst Nightmare is Coming True

Day'? Your daughter, Cassidy, will be hitting the roads behind the steering wheel in approximately one hour" I tease back at him.

Dad fakes a heart attack and then looks at me and smiles. Dad is hard not to like, witty and fun. I would say he is handsome, too. Not step out of a catalog handsome, but dark haired, blue eyed, fairly in shape, nice looking Dad-handsome.

"Nate, can you believe it?" Mom shrieks. "Our little girl is growing up. Pray for everyone on the roads today," Mom said trying to join in our banter. We tease her relentlessly about her failures to make a good come-back to our jokes, typically the equivalent of "No, you are." She looks happy today, but reflective. I know she doesn't really like the idea of me growing up.

Dad shakes his head with a smirk and continues putting on his shoes. I know he has to realize that Mom is secretly terrified about the thought of her first daughter driving, and not only, because of road hazards, but because it means I am edging ever closer to leaving the nest. Dad always has the ability to downplay things a little more than Mom ever could. She overthinks and worries enough for the both of them anyway. This is probably why Dad is my favorite parent as of late.

Mom and I don't have much time for breakfast, so we just grab a protein bar and head for the door. I open the garage, hop in mom's SUV, and say a prayer that I will pass the Driver's test, and let's be honest, also that my license picture will be good. I know that sounds superficial, but who doesn't want a good license picture? Mom and I wave good-bye to Dad and Charlotte who has now made her way down to the kitchen. The two of them have the gift of an extra fifteen minutes before their required departure. Charlotte smiles at us with a big grin filled with a mixture of big girl and baby teeth. I feel the nerves creeping up my stomach and can't even reciprocate her smile. But Dad is always guaranteed to get a smile out of me and lighten up the situation. He gives me a look like he is wilting until I smile and then he springs back up like a fresh, spring flower.

"Bye, Cass, Bye Ashley," Dad says with a wave, and we wave back, pulling out of the garage just like we do every day. And, it really seemed like the beginning of any perfectly, normal day. It was impossible for us to know that something, or someone rather, was making plans that threatened to change us, possibly forever.

Chapter Two—Him

The day is coming. I have planned and plotted and visualized every aspect of my entrance into the school. I have imagined their faces as they see mine. They would look confused, I'm sure. Initially, they would recognize my face and think I should be there, no big deal, they had seen me there often enough. But then, someone would realize that I wasn't supposed to be there anymore. I wasn't a student there any longer, and their faces would quickly change to show one of uncertainty, and then horror. Just the thought of it brought a smile to my face. Year after year, I had been a presence at that school, but could have very well been invisible to most. There were some who gave me a hard time which I hated and would stir a fire down deep inside me. I was too afraid to do much to stop them because I was smaller and quite honestly, outnumbered. The fire they started, continued to burn building slowly, but unstoppable nonetheless. Each day, being ignored, shoved off, dismissed, would be as if another log had been added to the fire and a slow burn became an inferno. A boiling point, really, that left no options. There was only one way to extinguish it, and that was to extinguish its' incubator. Me.

That was my plan at first. To go out on my birthday. I liked the full circle aspect of it. My birthday has pretty much always been a shitty day for me. At school, other kids would arrive to school on their birthdays and find their lockers decorated with notes, pictures, and glittery posters. They would be sung to at lunch acknowledging they were remembered and important. I have to admit, when I was younger, it stung. Of course, my parents would tell me happy birthday and even take me out to dinner, but it was not their attention I craved. I wanted to have that group of kids who sat at the same bench every day, who gave me a nickname, not a mean one, but a funny, familiar one, and as I got older, I wanted a girl to notice me. It didn't have to be the prettiest girl in school, but a girl who had all those things—the bench, the nickname, the laughter and the inside jokes with friends. I dreamed that she could pull me in, and I would be accepted because her status shone on me, too. It never happened.

Over time, my plan changed. If I just ended things, I would go out as I had lived—unknown. If I paid vengeance to those who had ignored me, I would never be unnoticed again. My name would be known and feared. I would be hated, but I wouldn't be invisible any longer.

Chapter Three—Cassidy

Success!! I cheered, as I left the DMV with a license in hand. Mom smiled her proud smile and offered to let me drive to school. I gladly grabbed the keys from her and hopped into the driver's seat. Luckily, we were still early and rush hour traffic hadn't begun, so I sailed to school with relative ease.

Once parked, Mom and I walked into North Franklin High and made our way to her office. You could tell she tried to make it inviting with all of the bright, sunny artwork. Most of it was stuff that Charlotte had made at school, on one wall she had pictures Charlotte had made of close-up sunflowers. They were meant to look like Georgia O'Keefe's famous paintings, but they looked like yellow blobs with brown blob centers. Mom had proudly labeled the bottom of them, one said "Charlotte, age four" at the bottom, and the other was aptly inscribed "Charlotte, age five". I know Mom was trying to show off her child's artistic genius at such a young age, I could read this woman like a book. She really couldn't be a prouder mom.

Across the office, on the other wall, hung Mom's degrees. She had her college degree from University of North Carolina proudly displayed, and then her School Counseling degree from Vanderbilt matted, and even more prominently positioned. I vaguely remember when Mom went back to school to get her degree from Vandy. She had been a stay at home mom for several years, so it was kind of strange not having her around to take us places all the time. We were always in some kind of carpool with Dad pitching in here and there. She was so proud when she graduated, and I remember her being one of the few graduates who had kids in the bleachers cheering as they walked across the stage in their caps and gowns. I was so proud of her in that moment, too. I had been her mini-me at the time. If anyone had ever asked me back then what I wanted to be when I grew up, I would have said a school counselor without hesitation, and followed that up with "and a Mom, of course". Mom always got a kick out of that.

There were a lot of funny stories about me being obsessed with her when I was little. I think that's one of the reasons why Mom has been having a hard time with me getting older. I used to think the sun rose and set on her, but now, I see her like a person. A nagging, overprotective, funny, good-hearted person who I don't want to spend every second with anymore. She of all people should know this. Wasn't that like her job? It was her business to know how teenagers are supposed to behave. I think it's pretty normal to want to hang out with your friends and not your own parents in high school, but Mom kept talking about how our relationship was strained. I could rarely resist an eye roll when she would start in on me with this topic. But the truth is, although I don't always show it, I know I got pretty lucky when it comes to parents. Some of my friends had parents who were never home, or would have no rules, or try to be cool, and really no one actually wants that. I never wanted my mom to have the cool factor.

I sat down on the couch in Mom's office while she worked on the computer waiting for her meeting to start. Each time I entered her office, I would make some reference to being psychoanalyzed or about Freud thinking I had daddy issues. Just as I was thinking of some Freudian reference, an all-too familiar voice broke in, and interrupted my train of thought. It was Mrs. Rosenblatt trying to herd the masses.

"All teachers and staff, please report to the cafeteria," her voice blared over the intercom.

"Hey Cass," Mom said, "I'm not going to be able to leave you in here while I'm gone. Too much confidential info, so you're going to have to come and sit outside the cafeteria and wait until the morning bell rings."

"Because I'm just dying to look at everyone's personal records," I said with an exasperated eye roll.

"Come on," Mom gestured to her door. Mom peeked out in the hallway to see if the masses were cooperating just yet, and they were, in fact, beginning to mosey down the hallway with coffee in hand. She turned out the lights in the Counseling Office and we made our way down the hall. The teachers and staff all filed into the cafeteria looking like a bunch of students—sluggish, dragging their feet, seemingly bored already, and annoyed that their planning time was cut short. Mom's friend, Mrs. Cooper, leaned over to her and said, "Hey, Ash, sit by me, so we can pass notes when it gets boring". I chuckled to myself and pictured them playing hang man in no time with words like tedious and superfluous.

"Cass, you can sit right outside here," Mom instructed me as she pointed to a table right outside the cafeteria doors with two chairs beside it.

"OK, I will just sit out here, and admire my new driver's license," I said with a grin. She grinned back at me and kept walking. I saw her and Mrs. Cooper enter together like me and Madison would do when we were forced into a school assembly or pep rally.

I could see pretty clearly into the cafeteria, so I watched as all of the teachers made their way in and found a seat. Several of them gave me a little nod as they entered. I knew a lot of them through being the counselor's daughter. Sometimes it had its' advantages, but most of the time, it was just awkward.

I noticed the teacher's lighthearted but annoyed moods quickly changed when they saw a man at the front of the room from the Safety department. He introduced himself as the head of School Safety, Mr. Bagwell. I leaned my head closer to the door because this seemed interesting and I didn't want to miss a thing.

Mr. Bagwell looked awfully serious as he watched each person enter the room and find their spot. His look was rather distinct, and just oozed 'ex-military'. His light brown hair was cropped close to his head with barely enough length to comb over on top. He wore a navy collared shirt that skimmed his abdomen tightly and was neatly tucked into his khakis. Not even the smallest bulge hung over his belt. Mr. Bagwell's face appeared stern with dark, narrow eyes and a strong chin. I wouldn't say he is an overly handsome man, but I could see where some teachers might find him appealing in that take-charge kind of way.

As he continued to wait for all of the stragglers to enter, his jaw remained tight, his brows were furrowed, and he continually looked around the room intently surveying every entrance and exit. The room remained completely silent. Our principal, Mr. Johnson, seemed to notice everyone's apprehension and quickly stood up to address the room.

Mr. Johnson did not have the same commanding presence as Mr. Bagwell, to say the least. Mr. Johnson was the kind of guy who would tell people he was 5'9", although he'd be lucky to measure up at 5'7", and that might even be generous. And, even though, Mr. Johnson couldn't impress with his physical presence, he certainly made up for it with his charisma, joking personality, and kind eyes. Mr. Johnson was truly beloved in Franklin. I know that's rare for a principal, but he was part of what made North Franklin great. He always knew when to come down hard on kids, or when they just needed some support. I bet he was like that with teachers, too. I could tell he was feeling the tension in the room. He stood up and looked around at each of the teachers, and began to speak to the crowded room with a reassuring tone.

"Teachers and Staff, I'm sure you have noticed Mr. Bagwell from the Safety Team has joined us today. There is no need to be alarmed, but there was an unsubstantiated threat made against our school. After a thorough investigation, the Safety Team believes it to be a prank. However, we are taking this opportunity to discuss lockdown procedures at our school. I will be turning the floor over to Mr. Bagwell for the rest of the meeting. Please give him your full attention."

OK, this was really weird, I thought to myself, *pranks, bomb threats, things like that had happened in the past, and I never remember them making a big deal out of it. He had their full attention, and mine, too, no doubt about that!*

"Thank you," Mr. Bagwell finally began, "as Mr. Johnson said, we are not currently under a threat, but we want to review lockdown procedures out of an abundance of caution. First, I want to talk about active shooters and how those are handled in our school system. As many of you may already know, the response to active shooters has changed dramatically since the days of the Columbine shooting" Mr. Bagwell said as he panned the room making eye contact with each person to underscore the seriousness of the topic.

"In the days of Columbine, the response was to secure the perimeter before entering a building, and to wait for the SWAT team to arrive. We now know that most killings within a school shooting are completed within the first six minutes of entering a building. There is no time to secure the building or wait for anybody. The School Resource Officer will sound the alarm to alert other safety personnel but will respond immediately and without back up to unarm or extinguish the active shooter. And yes, by extinguish, I mean shoot and kill," Mr. Bagwell once again stared at the concerned onlookers and squinted his eyes for dramatic effect.

"So, the question is, what will you do when this happens? Will you run around screaming and panicking? Will you curl up in a corner and wait for a gunman to find you? Or, will you stay calm and follow the protocol? Your answer better be the latter".

"When the code red alarm is sounded, you will close your door and lock it. You will cover the window with the posters that have been provided, so a shooter cannot see in your room. You will then begin barricading your door with desks and any items you can find to make it harder to enter. Finally, you will head towards the back of the classroom with your students, and stick together. Each student should have something in their hand that could be thrown at the intruder if entry is obtained. We are telling students to fight back now if they are in imminent danger. No longer is it just hide and wait. The world is changing and crazy people are looking for soft targets. The best chance of minimizing casualties is by disabling the shooter, sometimes, at any cost".

That sentence hung over the room like a lead balloon. What did he mean by at any cost? The truth is I knew he meant lives, kid's lives, teacher's lives, but it freaked me out to even think about it. I sneakily peeked around the room as I pretended to be reading, just in case Mom looked out to check on me. Some of the teachers looked shell-shocked. There were several teachers with tears in their eyes. *This is crazy*, I thought, *we live in a safe community, so it was doubtful this could ever really be our reality, but I guess there was always that slight possibility.*

Mr. Bagwell started in again, "And finally, something that will go against every grain in your conscience, but is vital to the safety of others. And remember, we are talking about minimizing casualties in these situations because we know there will be some. Absolutely under no circumstance should you unlock a locked door. Once your room is secured and the door is locked, you do not open it again until you see an officer enter your room. Now, I know you are thinking what if a student is outside and still trying to get somewhere securely. I'm telling you even if they are knocking on your door, you are not to open a locked door".

Yep, he was right. That would go against every instinct of a teacher or a counselor, or just a decent person, in general. I knew these teachers loved the kids at my school and wanted to help them—help them have a future. How could they ever leave a student stranded when they are looking at them for help? I was beginning to get really irritated with Mr. Bagwell for being so hard core.

Here he goes again. "And to sum it up, Mr. Bagwell stressed, I need to tell you something not as your Safety Team representative, but as your colleague. If this were to ever happen, you respond as you best can in the moment. Every one of you has a family yourself who want to see you come home at night. And every one of you has a right to live. In the end, respond the best way you know how, and pray that this never happens".

The teachers looked at each other in shock, and I felt like someone had punched me in the gut. This was unreal. These people, my mom, didn't choose professions in the police force,

19

or the military, they chose to be educators. It seemed crazy that these were the type of things they had to be prepared for nowadays.

"Thank you, Mr. Bagwell, we all appreciate the opportunity to brush up on the protocol," Mr. Johnson said. The teachers gave Mr. Bagwell an unenthusiastic clap and said thank you, but they looked like he had just dropped a bomb and left them there to deal with the aftermath. I don't know if I'd ever seen the teachers in my building so silent. They all began filing out of the cafeteria and back to our classrooms and offices. I pretended to be engrossed in my book, so I could avoid eye contact with any of them. Mom walked out of the meeting, and had a small look of panic on her face when she saw me and realized I had been there the whole time. She forced a smile on her face, and said, "Cass, did you hear any of that?"

"No, I was just reading my book and admiring my driver's license," I replied with a smile on my face.

I could tell she was in deep thought. Then, I noticed her shake her head as if she were trying to jostle the thoughts right out of her mind. If only it were that easy, for either one of us.

Chapter Four—Cassidy

Thoughts of the faculty meeting rose up throughout the day and into the evening, but I worked hard to suppress them. The next morning when the usual routine had begun once again, I had almost completely put them out of my mind. Just like normal, we were rushing to get ready, rushing to get breakfast, and rushing out the door. Mom hopped in the driver's seat, and I decided against begging for the opportunity to drive. I thought I would just enjoy looking at my phone and the chance to zone out.

Scrolling through my phone on the drive to school, I tuned out my mother's choice in music. Every now and then, I would hear her saying her daily prayer "Let me be the right person, in the right place, at the right time, to make a difference today". She used to say this daily on the way to school, but now, it would be like once a week, if she remembered. Today, she said it, and I couldn't resist giving her a side eyed glance. She smiled back at me, and I gave her an approving smirk in return. I have to admit, I did admire this woman for her sunniness if nothing else. I can't imagine doing the job she did every day. The kids at my school could be total jerks and she had to deal with the worst ones. You know the ones, the losers who were failing every class, getting into the wrong things, or just being jackasses in general.

Let me tell you, it's not fun thinking your mom is talking with people you know at your school. People would ask me about it sometimes, and I wanted to sink in a hole. You couldn't get anything past her either because she knew too much. She'd be like, "I know you said you were going to the movies tonight, but I heard that there was going to be a party in that new subdivision they're putting up". It was like the movies where the angel and the devil are sitting on the girl's shoulder, except Mom was the angel always in my ear.

I would dread the thought of running into her in the halls, and it does happen sometimes, even though I try to avoid it all costs. Sometimes, I swear she is doing it on purpose, too. Once in my freshman year, my boyfriend, Scott, broke up with me over text, and I just knew the world was ending. I cried for two hours straight in my room until Dad coaxed me out under the guise of needing my help with Charlotte's Math homework. The next day, Mom managed to casually be walking down the same hallway as me four different times. By the second time, I was glaring at her so hard I thought I would get a headache. She looked at me like "What? This is totally a coincidence," but I wanted to boot her back down to the Counseling Office, or better yet, back home! It's like she's obsessed with me!

Funny thing is that I used to be obsessed with her. I was the kid crying when I got dropped off at Mother's Morning Out. I cried at the church nursery, and the gym drop-off. My mom used to joke that she had made it to a record twelve minutes on the

Stair Master before they had to come get her. My mom was the kind of person who made you feel loved, I'll give her that. She was big on snuggling, and big on spending time together. We hit up the ice cream store more times than I could count. She'd get a coffee and I'd get ice cream. Mom was always watching her calories, even though she didn't really need to. She was a cute mom, not the hot kind... you know the ones with the giant, boobs, and the teenager-y clothes. She was more of the normal type mom. Fit for her age, dressed like a teacher trying to be a little hip, and smiling with really nice teeth. She said she'd gotten "Nicest Smile" as her Senior Superlative. I've seen pictures of her when she was younger, and she looked kind of like me—same blonde hair, same tan skin, but with a splattering of little freckles across her nose just like Charlotte.

One thing mom was big on was always seeing someone else's side. I remember it being really annoying when I'd vent to her about a friend, like Madison, who lived down the street. Madison was always fighting with me one second, and then making up with me the next. She'd get mad about the dumbest things. She'd say I didn't spend enough time with her at school, I was the teacher's pet, I should've worn the outfit she told me to wear to school so we could be twins. We were together all the time starting on the bus, during the day at school, and then on the bus home. If she was mad at me, the bus rides were brutal. There would be no speaking. I would slip her handwritten notes asking her why she was mad at me, and she'd act like I didn't exist. I would complain to my mom who would always tell me that Madison just thought of me as a sister, so that's why we fought more than some other friends. If it got really bad, Mom would tell me that I should be kind to Madison because maybe things weren't good for her at home. There was always some reason why Mom was telling me to be more understanding and to forgive. I wanted to scream back at her, "Maybe she's just a bitch, Mom." But, as it turns out, Mom was kind of right because Madison and I are like sisters and her dad ended up leaving her and her mom when we were kids. Things weren't so good at home, and they still aren't.

Our house kind of became a second home for Madison over the years. We were as close as two friends could be, more like sisters really. We fought like sisters, but had each other's back like sisters, too. In the looks department, though, we couldn't pass for cousins. Madison has long, dark, curly hair and mine is straight as a stick. Of course, we wish we could switch. Madison is tall and slender, but still has some curves. Honestly, her body is sick. If she weren't my best friend, I'd hate her. She has that exotic beauty thing going with olive skin and bright, green eyes. All the guys are crazy for Madison, and she's just as crazy for them. Even in elementary school, Madison was boy crazy. Everything I know about guys, I learned from her. She's taught me a lot, let's just say. Mom says Madison likes the attention of boys because she misses having the presence of a father figure. Mom is always psychoanalyzing everyone. But, I secretly think she might be right.

Madison has shared all of my major life moments with me. She's the first person I told when I started my period. We were in PE together in middle school, and I went to the bathroom and freaked. I screamed her name and let her into the stall with me. Cool as a cucumber, Madison talked me through everything. Of course, she'd already started her period and was an old pro now.

She seemed to always be a few steps ahead of me. Mom had not prepared me well for this moment. No pads in my purse, definitely no tampons, and no real idea of what the hell I was doing. Mom had given me some book when I started middle school about my changing body, and that was about it. She was like, "Ok, so you get why you need to wear deodorant, right?" For a counselor, she sure did like to avoid graphic topics. Luckily, Madison had everything I needed and made me feel like it was no big deal.

We were together the first time we got in BIG trouble. It was last year when we were freshmen. We told my mom that we were spending the night at Madison's house after the football game. After half time, we caught a ride with a few sophomores and went to a party. There was alcohol at the party, and we tried some beer. We just wanted to try and be rebels, I guess. We hung out at the party for a couple of hours, and then got dropped back off at the football stadium to get a ride to Madison's. It was the worst thing in the world to see my mom and dad standing outside of their car glaring at us. Mom and Dad had decided to come to the game at half-time to support the team (stalker!), and couldn't find us anywhere. Once they panicked, my friend, Taylor, had to tell them where we were. So, they knew we'd get dropped back off in time to be picked up by Madison's mom, and they just waited and waited. It was excruciating to face them and their disappointed looks. I was lectured for a solid two hours about lying and breaking their trust. I cried and told them I was sorry, but they kept saying they didn't know when they could trust me again. This has to be the line in the parent handbook under "Best way to make your child feel like a total dirt-bag". The worst part is I had done the unthinkable and embarrassed my mom in front of her co-workers. She said I had made her look like a fool because she was a counselor that couldn't even control her own kid. I saw her point, but it kind of pissed me off to think that was what she was the maddest about. I think this was when things starting going a little south for us.

Madison was there when Trey and I first started, too. I was taking Latin because Mom thought it would be the most helpful for the SAT. Always thinking ahead, that woman. Madison took it because I did. And, there were a few upperclassmen in the class who had finished out Spanish and were now taking Latin. I noticed Trey right away. He was really tall, not overtly hot, but nice looking and very well dressed. Most guys wore baggy basketball shorts and T-shirts to school, but Trey had on an untucked collared shirt, khaki shorts, and leather flip-flops. Preppy but laid back. He had a normal haircut, not the one with that obnoxious swoop in the front that guys were constantly pushing to the side. Just a nice, clean-cut look—brown hair with a slight wave to it, and deep brown eyes that seemed to invite you right in. He wasn't that chiseled pretty boy look that some girls like, but more the good ole Southern boy that knew how to treat a girl. Madison never would have been attracted to him. She went for bad boys all the way. Thank goodness we had different taste in guys because I don't think I could compete if Madison set her sights on Trey.

Funny thing is I didn't think he'd give me the time of day. Most seniors have one foot out the door and don't have time for lowly sophomores. I would sit and stare at the back of his head in class, and think, "Notice me. Notice me. Notice me." He never seemed to, so one day I built up the nerve to strike up a conversation with him.

"I think I heard them say your name on the announcements this morning," I said.

"Oh yea, they called out a bunch of seniors who had committed to colleges and where they're going," Trey explained.

"Where is it that you are going again?" I played dumb. I had heard every word, but I didn't want him to think I was taking that much notice.

"I committed to Wake Forest. I'm going to be on their golf team," Trey stated rather proudly.

"Congratulations, Trey," I said with a smile.

And so it began, small, superficial interactions that grew more frequent and more in-depth by the day. I noticed everything about him. He had a small little dimple on the right side of his face, full lips for a guy, a warm smile that literally could make my heart skip a beat, and a mouth full of white, straight teeth that only looked whiter next to his tan skin. He spent a lot of hours on the golf course, and you could see he sported a nice, little tan line where his socks would have been. He was lean, not built, but his tanned arms had those lines of definition from hours of swinging a golf club. And, his voice was deep with the smallest touch of a southern accent which I loved, and just made him seem that much more genuine.

Then, right before Thanksgiving Break, something changed

for us. We normally talked briefly as we got to class before the bell rang. We would talk about what we were doing over the weekend, or if we had studied for the test, that kind of thing. As much as I hung on his every word, I didn't think there would ever be a chance that he might possibly like me in that way. But, he said we should exchange phone numbers in case we ever forgot something for class. I was shocked. Did Trey really just ask me for my phone number? It was probably nothing, just like he said, just for studying. So, I put his number in my phone, too. Madison was staring at us with one eyebrow raised and a smile on her face. She knew I thought Trey was perfection. I just couldn't get into the guys that were in my grade for some reason. I'd known them since we were little, and they were still kind of immature. But, Trey was different—mature, but funny, driven, and nice (I mean he was being extra nice to some sophomore girl he happened to sit by in Latin). We left class that day, and I said a little prayer for him to make contact with me. At this point, I would take a text asking me if I knew what the homework assignment was.

But, it got better than that. Over the break, I got a text from Trey.

"Salve. Happy Thanksgiving."

Cute, he said hello in Latin. I didn't know if I should text back right away, or play it cool. Forget that, I thought.

"Hey," lame, I know, but I was dying.

"Do you want to get together over the break?"

"Volens et potens " A little Latin right back at him. 'Willing and able', now, that was an understatement. I was feeling pretty satisfied with that response.

"Can I pick you up at 7:00?"

Yes, but no, I knew Mom would have none of me leaving the house in a car with a senior, so I texted, "Sure, I'll be at Madison's. I'll text you the address."

"Sounds good, and wear comfortable clothes."

"Can't wait." I didn't care what we were doing because I would have gone anywhere with him.

Chapter Five—Trey

The absolute last thing I wanted was to find a girlfriend in my senior year of high school. It just didn't make sense. I would be leaving Charlotte and heading to Winston Salem in the fall. It's not that far, but I didn't want any ties to hold me back. I'd only had one serious girlfriend in my life and it was a major distraction. Golf had been my girlfriend for the most part, so I could get a scholarship. I played nine holes every day afterschool, spent hours on the driving range and the putting green. I had endless hours of private coaching worked into my schedule, and on top of that, I still had to keep my grades up to get into a good school. And now, I was reaping the rewards. I had done everything I had set out to do. I had gotten a thick packet from Wake Forest University with an acceptance on my early decision application. Life was moving along as planned. That was the case, until out of nowhere, I met a girl worth getting distracted for, Cassidy Maxwell.

I noticed Cassidy on the first day of school. She came into Latin class with her friend, and they were laughing hysterically about something. She was the kind of girl who drew your eye to her with her All-American good looks. I pretty much summed them up as silly, sophomore girls at the time.

Each day, though, I noticed more about her. For one, she was smart, and she tried. She listened, took notes, and asked questions in class. She seemed to have a confidence about her, not hesitating to raise her hand and speak to the teacher. On her way out of class, she would say, "Bye, Mr. Holley. Thank you" or "Have a good day". She was polite, not the typical teenage kid, just racing out the door as fast as they could. If someone missed class, she'd offer to let them copy her notes. She spoke to a lot of the people in class not just her friend, Madison. She could be funny, too. Some days, she'd exit the classroom with a message of "Carpe Diem" to Mr. Holley. He'd chuckle and reply, "And you, Carpe Noctum". Cassidy would laugh, and Madison would exclaim, "Seize the Night". Cassidy Maxwell became more and more attractive to me with each passing day. Finally, at the beginning of November, she spoke to me, and that was all it took to break the ice.

We started talking to each other every day, and then, I finally got up the nerve to ask her for her phone number. I said it was for school reasons, just to play it safe. When I finally asked Cassidy out, and she said yes, I knew I had to make it a memorable night. I worked out a plan and spent the rest of the day getting the materials, making everything, and setting it up to surprise her. By the time I left to pick her up at Madison's, I had already spent hours on making this a perfect date. I had never tried like this for a girl. Something about her, made me want to.

When I picked up Cassidy, she waved a quick good-bye to Madison and I opened the door for her to jump in my Toyota

4Runner.

"I like your car," Cassidy said with a timid smile.

   "Thanks, I bought it from my dad when I got my driver's license. It's usually a mess with golf stuff everywhere, but I got it cleaned today for you," I said trying to impress her.

She smiled at me, and said, "So, I've been dying to know, where are you taking me? Should I be worried?"

"Not at all, we'll be there in less than five," I reassured her.

As we pulled up to my house, she looked a little concerned.

"Don't worry, I'm not making you meet the parents just yet," I teased. We parked and I took her on the side path from the driveway to my backyard.

"Trey, your home is beautiful," she said enthusiastically. "Now, I can see why you are such a good golfer. I didn't realize you actually lived on the golf course."

"Yea, we're on the twelfth hole. I've been walking these holes with my dad since I was four. My favorite playground when I was kid," I confessed.

As we walked up to the course, Cassidy could see the scene I had staged for us, and she jumped up and down.

"Trey, this is amazing! It must have taken you forever to set this up," Cassidy exclaimed.

"Oh, this? It was nothing... I just handmade a mini golf course for us, out of milk cartons, cardboard boxes, and soda bottles." I gave her a squeeze on her shoulder and said, "Well, how else was I going to check out your skills."

Cassidy ran around noticing every detail. The perimeter of the golf course was lined with mason jars filled with sand, with small candles inside. There were five golf holes made of plastic bottles with the bottoms cut off of them, and arches cut into them, each labeled with the numbers one to five. Off to the side in the trees, hung a double hammock with two lanterns nearby. Not far from the hammock, lay a blanket with a large, linen bag on top, and two candlesticks.

"Trey, I am really impressed," she exclaimed.

"You should be," I said in the most flirtatious way possible. "You hungry?"

"That's a silly question. I'm always hungry," she said with a grin.

I grabbed Cassidy's hand and led her over to the blanket. I had picked up Italian food from her favorite restaurant, Piccini's. I had overheard Madison and Cassidy talking about it one day in class and had purposely filed that information away for later use.

"Trey, I'm beginning to think you are too good to be true," Cassidy said as she looked at me mildly questioning.

"Cassidy, you haven't seen anything yet," I said, subtly promising there would be more dates to come.

As we ate dinner, I know we talked about our families, school, the teachers we liked, and the ones that bored us to death, but to be honest, it was all a little foggy. I was caught up in Cassidy's eyes, and the adorable look that she made when she feigned surprise, and her beautiful, smile that was absolutely addicting to me.

After dinner, Cassidy and I walked over to what I called "the entertainment portion of the evening". I handed Cassidy a putter and told her there was a small catch to the game. Each time one of us putted through the hole, we would have to draw a card from the stack of cards in the middle of the pseudo putting green I had created. Each card had a question on it that we'd both have to answer.

"I'm game," Cassidy exclaimed, "let's do this!"

Cassidy's golfing ability left much to be desired which had her laughing like crazy. She three putted the first hole by barely tapping the ball the first time, overcompensating and knocking the ball clear across the green, and finally dropping the ball right in front of the hole and tapping it through the arch.

"Wow," I said, "that was creative."

She gave me a gingerly punch on the arm, and began laughing hard. She even had little tears in her eyes. I, of course, had to show off and get a hole in one, to which she squealed, "Show off!!"

"Ok, Cassidy, time to draw a card," I directed.

"Got it," she said as she slid a card off the top of the deck. "The first question is…." she paused, and then teased, "drumroll, please." I complied with the obligatory drumroll. "What makes you smile?"

Cassidy thought for a minute, and then said "So many things, but if I had to name one, I would say boys with dimples." And when she said it, she had a look of wanting that I almost couldn't resist.

"Good one," I said, "and, for me, I would have to say, girls who know Latin."

"Well, you know what I always say about me and mini golf," she laughed, "Veni, Vidi, Vici"!

"You came, yes, you saw, yes, but conquered? We'll see about that," I goaded.

We moved on to the second hole, and after several attempts, and more fits of laughter, Cassidy putted her ball through again. She drew another card.

"Let's see, question number two…What terrifies you the most?" she said contemplatively. "This one is kind of deep, let me think." After a minute or so, Cassidy hesitated but then replied, "Well, not to get too heavy, but I've always been absolutely terrified something bad was going to happen to someone I love.

I had separation anxiety when I was little, and would always worry that my mom would get into an accident or something."

"Aw, I hope you've gotten over that now" I said optimistically.

"No, actually, I haven't," Cassidy confided, "it's weird, but I guess we all have our quirks."

I loved that she wasn't afraid to be honest with me. I reached over and put my arm around her. I looked at her blue, soulful eyes, and wanted to lean in for a kiss, but lost my nerve.

"Ok, my turn," I said to redirect us. "I'm absolutely terrified of spiders." We laughed, and Cassidy snapped right back to being her fun-loving self.

Cassidy grabbed the putter for the third hole and proceeded to tap the ball very lightly not once but three times. By the third tap, she had successfully gotten the ball through the arch of the milk carton. She launched into a celebration dance, and then beamed at me with a smile that went all the way up to her eyes.

"Top that," she challenged me.

"I don't know if I can, but I'll try," I said mockingly. I decided to give Cassidy a break and four putted the hole using her tap-tap-tap-tap method.

"You win that hole," I said with a smirk.

Cassidy went to give me a high five, and I held her hand tight.

We sat there for a moment, looking at each other, holding hands, and my heart pounded so loudly, I thought she could hear it. I can't describe the feeling she gave me. It was like complete fullness, like I was brimming over. I leaned in and gave her a kiss on the cheek. Cassidy blushed and looked down demurely. I reached for the question cards to distract myself from what I really wanted to do.

"Ok, question number three, what is your biggest goal in life?" I asked, as I looked at her with honest interest.

"Um, OK, this is going to sound so unoriginal, but I've always wanted to do something heroic. I want to be remembered for something good," Cassidy replied with the most earnest expression.

"And, I have no doubt you will, Ms. Cassidy Maxwell," I reassured her.

"New question for you, Mr. Trey Buchanan...if you can handle it... What is your biggest turn off, if guys even have one?" Cassidy said with genuine curiosity.

"Ladies first," I said with a slight nod of the head.

"Oh, that's an easy one for me," Cassidy said, "arrogance." Cassidy continued, "I can't stand guys, or girls, actually, who act better than other people. It's like, just humble yourself, you know? But, don't think you're getting out of this one, what is your turn off, Trey?"

"I don't really have one," I joked.

"Typical," Cassidy said with a pretend look of disgust.

"I kid, I kid. I do, believe me. I'd have to say girls who lack substance. They're all over school. Just all about how they look, fake, you know the ones I'm talking about, right? You're not at all like them, Cassidy, you're real, you're kind...I could tell that when I first met you." I said sincerely.

"Trey, I knew you were different, too. I didn't think you'd give me a second glance, though." Cassidy confessed and then grabbed my hand again.

I grabbed her around the waist and leaned in for a kiss while pulling her up towards me. She stood on her tiptoes and our mouths met. It was, at first, just a kiss, and then, it was hot. I pressed Cassidy as close as I could until I could feel our breathing become in synch. I wanted to keep this going for the rest of the night, but I wanted her to feel comfortable. I was well aware that she was just sixteen. I pulled away slightly, and said, "Ok, I concede, you came, you saw, and now, you have conquered me."

I don't really remember how, but we quickly ended up lying together in the hammock, alternating between kissing, looking up at the stars, and laughing. I couldn't shake the feeling that things were going too perfectly. Nothing had ever been this effortless for me. I was always trying harder, working to meet my dad's ever-increasing expectations, not ever taking my eye off the ball out of fear. But, in this moment, nestled perfectly against me, lay my soothing remedy, and I couldn't get enough of her.

Chapter Six—Madison

Cassidy and I have been friends for forever. She tells me everything, so I knew how crazy she was about Trey. When he asked her out, she immediately called me. The night of their big date, we picked out her outfit with precision—not too dressy but not too casual, cute, but kind of outdoorsy. We finally settled on jeans, boots, and a flannel shirt, with a slim, grey puffer vest. She looked so good with natural make up, brown eyeliner, and sheer, pink lip gloss. When Trey came to the door, I sent her off like a proud parent.

I heard the car pull up again around midnight, and peered out the window. Trey opened the car door and walked Cassidy up to my front porch. I saw him go in for a kiss, and quickly closed the blinds. A few minutes later, Cassidy opened the door breathless. She closed the door behind her, leaned against it, and put her hand on her heart with the biggest grin that I'd ever seen.

I had to laugh at her, but secretly I was thrilled to see her like this. It was rare to see her this excited about a guy. Honestly, the only boyfriend I could ever remember her having was Scott, and he was a jerk.

"So, how was it, or need I ask?" I joked.

"Oh, Mads, it was beyond perfection, he's beyond perfection, we're beyond perfection," Cassidy exclaimed.

I pressed Cassidy for every detail and she more than complied sparing not a single morsel. And, we giggled together for hours. I can't deny it; Trey was quite the catch. A nice guy who seemed like he really knew how to treat a girl. Of course, being the overprotective friend, I worried that she was setting herself up for heartbreak, since he was graduating in six months. Even with my worries, I could never detract from her moment tonight. She was positively glowing, and I was eating up the romantic story play by play.

I really didn't realize that this was the beginning of Cassidy and Trey becoming completely inseparable. Even though I missed having Cassidy more to myself, they always did their best to include me. They were the kind of couple who made some people sick. He would meet her at her locker first thing in the morning, leaning in to her as they talked. Sometimes, I would sneak up and squeeze in between them to get a laugh. They would laugh and then go right back to gazing at each other as they spoke. From what I could tell, they wouldn't even be talking about anything that important, but Cassidy hung on his every word. If Trey wasn't such a good guy, I would honestly be jealous, and I still kind of was, but Cassidy deserved this, and I knew it.

Cassidy's mom wasn't really going for the senior/sophomore thing. I love Mrs. Maxwell, I really do, but the woman could really be a killjoy sometimes. I got it, though. Mrs. Maxwell was all about protecting Cassidy. She didn't do it to be mean and unfair, even I could see that that was the case. She did it out of pure love as suffocating as that can be. Cassidy would complain about it a lot. I knew her mom was really like her biggest role model, but she'd always say that her mom was like cling wrap, snugly attached and keeping everything perfectly contained. Cassidy knew the quickest way to make her mom irate was to embarrass her because her image was that she had everything under control.

I have like the exact opposite situation at my house. My mom is like re-experiencing her youth or something. After my dad walked out on us when I was seven, she changed. She was really bitter for a while and she had to work a lot to pay the bills. Then, she started going out with friends, guys, whoever. I love my mom because she's my mom, and I know she loves me, too, but we're more like friends. Sometimes, I'm even the more mature friend.

I spend a lot of time at Cassidy's house because they have like the family thing going on. They have dinner together most of the time. It's not like the perfect family dinner you see on TV, and Mr. Maxwell is only there half the time because he works late, but I still like it. Mrs. Maxwell says she's an "add-on cook". She takes something store-bought and adds to it. We laugh because sometimes her additions are improvements and sometimes they are just gross. We also do this thing at their house called "Rose, thorn, and bud". Each person goes around the table and says their rose, what went well that day, their thorn, what didn't go well, and their bud, what they're looking forward to. It sounds totally corny, but we all like it, especially Cassidy's sister, Charlotte. That kid is my kryptonite. I've known her since she was born, and I cannot refuse her anything.

Sometimes, I just stay later and talk to Mrs. Maxwell. She really is a good listener. She always tells me things to encourage me. She tells me that I'm the most self-sufficient person she knows, and it will serve me well in life. I think she's trying to comfort me for not having my folks around much, but I'll take it as a compliment. She calls me her third daughter. I have had a lot of memorable moments at their house. I got ready before Homecoming at their house so Cassidy's mom could help with my hair and take pictures of us. I know my mom would like to do these things, too, but she's usually working because she always picks up a shift if she can.

I wish Cassidy knew how lucky she was sometimes. I would give anything to have a mom who would actually tell me I couldn't do something because she'd be too worried about me. Sometimes I have a hard enough time getting my mom to even notice me. For as much as my mom says men are the worst and there are no good men out there, she sure spends an awful lot of time trying to meet one.

I've dated lots of guys... no one really special. They come and go, just like mom says they do. Someday, I want what Cassidy and Trey have, but I don't know if that will ever happen to me. I think I might be damaged because of my dad. I usually cut bait when I'm dating someone before they have a chance to. I've never been dumped because I'm out of there too quickly.

The only people I really have that I can count on are Cassidy and her family. It sounds weird because we're not even blood family. I would do anything for them and they'd do anything for me. I think that's what family really is when you think about it.

Chapter Seven—Cassidy

After Trey and I had our first date, we didn't spend another day apart for the next four months. I finally had to tell my parents about him. My dad was all about it because he loves golf and thought it was so cool that Trey got a golf scholarship to Wake Forest. My mom, on the other hand, thought it was strange that a seventeen-year-old who was about to graduate would start dating a sophomore girl. She made her distrust very well-known and reminded me often that Trey would be graduating soon. I didn't really feel comfortable having my mom around me and Trey that much. Luckily, I still had Madison's as a way to get to see Trey, or if we had to, we would hang out at my house, or even at Trey's.

Trey's parents weren't too excited about the idea of him getting a girlfriend either. I overheard his dad talking to him one day about it when he didn't know I was there. He was telling him that he had worked too hard to lose focus, and that he liked me just fine, but I was a distraction. Trey told him that losing me would be worse than losing everything, and I wanted to cheer from the other room. I had never felt this way before. I know it sounds crazy and very love-struck teenager, but I really could see us going the distance. We hadn't talked about what was going to happen when he left in the fall, but there was absolutely no indication we would be breaking up.

Things continued to be a little tense at home. Mom and I would fight because she wanted me to spend more time with the family. Then, she and Dad would fight because he'd tell her to let me be. Mom obviously couldn't remember what it was like to be in love. All I could do was think of Trey and nothing else. When I wasn't with Trey, he was constantly in my thoughts. Sometimes I would even feel like I was in physical pain, when I couldn't see him.

After Trey hit golf balls afterschool, he would either stop by my house or see if we could go out for some frozen yogurt or just hang out. After a few months of dating, Trey texted me on his way home from the practice range, and asked if he could pick me up and take me back to his house. Just the thought of being alone with him made my stomach fill with butterflies and longing. I peeked downstairs to see if Mom was home yet. She had to stay at school late that day for a meeting so Dad was there in his office on a conference call. I snuck down quickly and mouthed to Dad, "heading to Madison's." He nodded in agreement and waved me off. I felt bad to lie, but Mom didn't let me go off with Trey by myself. I'm sure she was afraid we'd get physical. Little did she know, I was dying to get physical. I could kiss Trey for hours.

I ran out to meet Trey on the street and hopped in his car, hoping Dad didn't notice. As soon as I was safely inside, I leaned in for kiss. Trey was the best kisser. Not the kind that was sloppy and wet, but the passionate kind where it felt like it would lead to taking things much further, but we didn't allow it to.

We drove to his house and hung out in the basement alternating between watching TV together and making out. Trey would lay on top of me and I could feel each breath he took. We would start to breathe in synchronicity and it felt like we were attached. Trey stared into my eyes and put his hands on the sides of my face.

"Cass," he started, "I have never been this happy before. This time with you has meant the world to me."

I listened for a but, my biggest fear was that he was going to tell me that as much as he liked me, it just didn't make sense for us to get serious. *Well, too late for that*, I thought. I was in this all the way, and there was no way to slow it down.

"Trey, I'm really happy, too," I concurred. I waited anxiously for his response, and once again, held my breath, afraid that this conversation would take a turn for the worse.

Trey continued, "My dad just doesn't understand what I'm doing with you. He thinks this is just some senior fun, but it isn't, Cassidy. I've never felt like this about anyone."

I breathed a big sigh of relief and started to feel tingly everywhere. So, this is what love feels like. It felt all-consuming. It felt worth the risk of getting into trouble, worth the risk of defying our parents, and even worth the risk of getting my heart broken.

47

"Cassidy Maxwell, I wanted to tell you that I'm falling in love with you, but the truth is, I've already fallen. I am in love with you," Trey boldly stated and held me tightly.

"I love you, too, Trey," I replied and I gave him a kiss, and then another, and then another.

When Trey dropped me back off at my house, Mom was standing in the foyer waiting for me. I started freaking out. Reality had set in, and I was going to have to pay the price for my little jaunt off with Trey. Truth is, it was worth it. I knew Mom was going to be so mad that I had lied. Lying made her madder than anything else. I tried to come up with a quick story. I hurriedly jumped out of Trey's 4-Runner, so he would be long gone before her wrath was unleashed.

I walked in the door and braced myself. Mom had an angry look on her face as she stood there glaring at me with her hands on her hips. I looked at her meekly.

"Cassidy Leigh Maxwell," Mom screamed, "you are caught red-handed." Mom started in again, "we figured out pretty quickly that you weren't at Madison's when she called here looking for you."

"I'm sorry, Mom, I didn't want to worry you. Trey and I just needed to talk so we drove around for a little while," I explained. "I just knew you wouldn't like me being with Trey alone, but you need to realize we are getting serious. We love each other."

"Cassidy, please, you don't even know what love is yet. What you and Trey have is called infatuation. And, I don't want you getting all caught up in the emotion of the moment and doing something you'd regret, young lady," Mom hammered on unrelenting.

"Mom, I can't believe you. You don't understand anything. Don't you remember what it was like to be young and in love? Probably not, because it's been so long and you probably never felt like this about anyone, even Dad," I said and kind of regretted it because it looked like I wounded her. I think I hit a nerve talking about Dad.

"Cassidy, I don't want to look at you right now. Go to your room. And, call Madison back because she sounded like she had been crying when she called, or have you quit being there for her, too?" Mom questioned harshly.

"Gladly," I countered, "and that was a low blow, Mom." I stormed up the stairs and threw myself on my bed. That woman could infuriate me like no other. The worst part of fighting with your mom is how you end up feeling guilty about it. My thoughts kept wandering over to her side of the fight, I knew I had disobeyed her rules, but I wouldn't have to if she wasn't so strict, I rationalized. But, within no time, I would start feeling bad again. I hated arguing with her.

I grabbed my phone, and called Madison. She always made me feel better. "Hey, Mads, it's me," I said softly.

"Cass, thank God you're home, things are really bad, and I didn't know who to call," Madison said through tears.

49

"I'm here for you, I promise," I comforted her and reassured myself.

Chapter Eight—Madison

I had to reach Cassidy, she would know what to do. I walked in the door afterschool into an empty house, nothing unusual about that. Mom was typically working a double shift or out with some guy most of the time. She had actually been kind of dating the same guy for a couple of months. I didn't care for him. When Mom introduced us, he gave me an uneasy feeling. First of all, he shook my hand and held onto it really tightly and for a longer time than was normal. Yuck! Secondly, he leered at me with an unnerving stare like he liked what he saw a little too much. Mom had the worst taste in men, I swear.

Suddenly, I heard a noise coming from Mom's bedroom. I felt a little scared because I thought I was alone, but I walked quietly in that direction to check it out. It was a muffled sound coming from the closet. Before I opened the door, I went over to the side of Mom's bed and picked up the baseball bat that she left there for protection. I tried to calm my fears by convincing myself that it was probably just the cat somehow accidentally stuck in the closet. I reached for the doorknob, and fell backwards in shock as our cat actually sprung out from underneath the bed.

"Damn, Tinkerbell, you scared the hell out of me." I screamed at the cat. Once again, I attempted to open the closet door. I heard the muffled sound again of a quiet whimpering. I opened the door carefully with the bat in hand.

There sat Mom all curled up in a ball. Her lip was puffy and bleeding and her left eye was bruised and swollen. She looked to be in a lot of pain.

"Mom! Are you OK? What happened to you?" I grilled her. I went in the closet and sat beside her. "Are you in pain?"

"I'm OK. I didn't want you to see me like this. I hoped you wouldn't know I was here," Mom explained.

"Seriously, what happened? Who did this to you? Was it a robber? Did someone break in?" I probed compassionately.

"It was Steve, but I don't want you to hate him. He's a good guy, but just has a bad temper, and we got into a bad argument. It was probably my fault. I wouldn't let up," Mom said trying to defend her lowlife boyfriend.

"You can't be serious. That's it. He better not even show his face around here again. I'm calling the police," I threatened but was deadly serious.

"No, Madison, no, you can't," Mom begged. "It won't happen again, he promised."

"Mom, do you have any idea how pathetic you sound right now?

You are better than this. You deserve better than this jerk." I cried trying to convince her.

"Madison, I can handle this," Mom declared, "but I do appreciate your concern. Can you help me get up and get into my bed?"

I knew it was no use. We had been down this road before. Mom just couldn't walk away from a man. My dad had really done a number on her confidence by walking out on us.

I helped Mom up and pulled down the covers on her bed. I helped her ease into her bed and went to get an ice pack for her eye. I turned on the TV for her for background noise, and turned her overhead light out, so she could get some rest. Once I had her situated, I went to my room and screamed. I threw my books, slung everything off my desk, and broke down in tears on the floor. I reached for my phone to call my other half, Cassidy, she'd know what to do.

I called her only to be told that she wasn't home. Surprise! I'm sure she was off with Trey somewhere. I flung myself onto my bed and cried hard. I cried that deep cry that comes straight from the bottom of your soul and feels unstoppable. I cried for my mom but I cried for myself, too. I cried about my dad leaving us, I cried about not having a "normal" family, I cried about having to be the grown up in my house. I sobbed so hard my head ached. I wanted to be enough for my mom. Why couldn't I be enough to make her happy?

Just when I thought I couldn't muster up another tear, my phone rang. It was Cass. I filled her in, and she did what she always did. She listened to me, really listened to me, and reassured me that everything was going to be alright.

"Cassidy, promise me one thing," I begged, "promise me, that we'll always be together. You won't leave me, right?"

"Never, Mads. Never," Cassidy reassured me.

I may not have lucked out in the parent department, but I really lucked out in the friend department. Cassidy was the only person on this Earth that really knew me, and still loved me. I would do anything for her, too. I thought about that quote you always hear about friends, "Friends are the family you choose." Cassidy was my family.

Chapter Nine—Cassidy

By the next morning, Mom's fury had lessened. I thought it would be best to avoid talking to her unless I had to. I got ready for school quickly without having to be prodded. We rode to school together without saying much. As we got out of the car, Mom grabbed my arm and stopped me.

"I miss the old Cassidy," she said.

"Oh, Mom, not now," I groaned.

"Really. I want to spend some quality time together," Mom asserted not letting this one slide.

"OK, Mom, we will soon. Got to go," I said as I walked away briskly.

Mom still had a way of coaxing me into spending time with her. We would either go shopping or go on walks to 'stay close' as she liked to say. I felt a walk n' talk coming on soon. And I was right, Mom found me in my bedroom afterschool, and urged me to go on the four-miler with her. I agreed, just to make peace more than anything.

This time, she asked about Trey and Madison and all the typical things, but then she starting talking to me about the faculty meeting I'd overheard at school on my birthday. It really freaked me out because I had tried to put it out of my mind. I was kind of surprised Mom even brought it up because she usually liked to shield me from what she would call 'negativity'.

Mom started rehashing the safety meeting. I think she just needed to process it with someone. She said the head of the Safety Department had called an emergency meeting with the faculty because there had been an anonymous threat received at the school. She reassured me and I think herself, too, that they had investigated but found the threat to be unwarranted. However, just to be on the safe side, they planned a mandatory review of the lockdown procedures at the school. This was all raising my anxiety again as I pretended to be hearing all of this for the first time.

"Mom," I asked, "if they don't think the threat is real, then why would they take all of these precautions?" Mom assured me that it was just what they do in school systems, and I didn't need to worry. *A little too late for that*, I thought.

The interesting thing was Mom reiterated what they had told them about never opening a locked door in a school lockdown. I was like "Well, Duh, Mom," but she said this would be really hard for her. She went on to talk about how this would even be true if there were students standing at the door needing to come in. I couldn't bear the thought of my mom being in this situation. I knew she'd never be able to leave someone out in the hallway in danger. I tried to get her off the subject, but she seemed to really need to talk it out with someone. She also said they told them that everyone has the right to live, and they wouldn't be held accountable for what they did in a moment of survival. She had really started to upset me. I could feel my heart rate quickening as I visualized this possibility. Although rare, Mom and I had a discussion that didn't include her usual layer of protection.

"Mom," I said, "do you think this could ever happen at our school?"

"No," she calmed me, "I don't, honey, but sadly, every school that has ever had a shooter would have said the same thing. It's not something you could ever plan for, totally. If this were to ever happen at our school, I would just have to pray for God to lead me".

"Ok, Mom, now you are really killing me. Stop talking like this. Do you know something?" I demanded an answer.

"I do not know of any threat", Mom stated firmly, "It's just on my mind lately because of the meeting. Some of the teachers actually had tears in their eyes. We talked about past school shootings and what they'd done right and what they'd done wrong, so we could be better prepared if it ever happened. I just couldn't imagine."

"Well, then, let's not, Mom," I said abruptly, "I can't think of anything bad happening to you or anyone in our family."

Mom stopped dead in her tracks and pulled me in for a long, hug. She held me tight right there in the middle of the sidewalk. I thought of pulling away, but then I hugged her back. It had been a long time, since I'd openly showed affection to anyone but Trey. I just felt like she needed that hug and truthfully, I did, too. I said in that moment what I felt needed to be said.

"I love you, Mom," and gently pulled out of the hug. Mom smiled with gladness and she replied with her typical answer.

"And, I love you a bushel and a peck," she said with an expectant smile.

"And a hug around the neck," I said with a pretend look of irritation this time, but she knew I was kidding.

The school safety discussion seemed so far removed from our reality. I had never felt the least bit threatened at my school. I couldn't get it entirely out of my mind, though. I couldn't completely quit thinking about the look on Mom's face as she talked about it. It was a look of concern but also a look of resolve that she didn't usually show, or at least not that I had ever noticed before. It wasn't long before every scenario, every 'should', every standard protocol we discussed was right before us, and just like Mom warned, no one saw it coming.

Chapter Ten—Charlotte

April showers bring May flowers, and standardized testing at school. Blech. It's testing day at school. Yuck. Daddy woke me up this morning, and I pretended to fall back to sleep. He started off with a sweet, little pat on the head, telling me it was time to get up. Then, he returned with a meaner tone telling me to hurry and get up. So, I did.

We are having the end of the year tests at school, and I hate those days. BOOOORRRING! I hurried to get ready, though, because Daddy always makes me special breakfasts on those mornings. It is always something that has high protein or brain food as he calls it, but I like it because it usually involves bacon or sausage. Yummy! They call me "The Baconator" at my house because I love it so much.

I could hear Mommy and Cassidy grabbing something fast to eat downstairs. Mommy was telling her to at least grab one of the protein bars, and that they had to hurry since there would be testing today. Cassidy and Mommy are always rushing out the door to get to school together since they go to the same school every day. I will be a North Franklin Falcon one day myself. My school North Franklin Elementary goes to North Franklin Middle and then to North Franklin High. I want to be like Cassidy when I get to high school. Cassidy is super pretty. She is usually nice to me. I know I bug her sometimes, but that is what little sisters do, am I right?

My favorite is Madison! She is at our house a lot. I love to play with her. She calls me Char, and always gives me hugs. She always tells me I'm the coolest third-grader she knows. She will braid my hair for me if I ask, and she does it really good and really tight, like I like it, with no wispies hanging out. I like to sleep in it, and then take it out the next morning for wavy hair. She will listen to my stories about school and won't tell me to get out if she and Cassidy are hanging out. Cassidy always says that I need to let them have girl talk and I need to leave.

I also love to hang out with Mommy. She and I have a routine for Wednesday nights. We call it Wacky Wednesday. After she picks me up from cheer, we swing by Wild Bill's Burgers on the way home and pick up food for everybody. I always get the same thing—a cheeseburger, with mayo, mustard, and ketchup, hold the onions and the pickle. For the past few months, Trey comes over for Wacky Wednesday. He always gets a Wild Bill Original Burger with the works and onion rings. I guess he's not worried about having onion breath. He should be, though, because he and Cassidy are always a little kissy-kissy after dinner.

Trey is super handsome. I kind of have a crush on him, too. He always calls me Little Maxwell. He will sometimes play hide and seek with me. It's hard for him to hide because he's so tall, but wherever I hide, it takes him forever to find me. I can always hear his footsteps pounding my way, and I get little butterflies in my stomach when I hear him coming. When he finally says "Gotcha", he swoops me up and give me some tickles. It's super fun.

I'm excited for Wacky Wednesday tonight. Daddy is there sometimes if he can get home in time. If he works late, Mommy wraps up his burger and sticks it in the fridge and puts a sticky note on it. Sometimes it will say something like wake me up when you get home or sometimes it just has a heart on it.

Speaking of Daddy, he's screaming at me from downstairs that I need to come down. I can't be late today because we will go immediately into the testing. Wacky Wednesday should really be called Worry Wednesday today because everyone is worried about eating the right breakfast, being at school on time, and doing well on the tests. As I run down the stairs, Daddy is holding two pencils in his hand. He tells me they are lucky pencils for the test. I laugh at him because I know there is no such thing as lucky pencils. Daddy is such a goofball.

We hop in Daddy's car to head to the carpool line. Right as Ms. Gables is about to open the car door to let me out, Daddy tells me he loves me a bushel and a peck and I reach up from the backseat and give him a hug around the neck. Into school I go, but I turn around a give Daddy one last wave, and he grins at me.

Chapter Eleven—Trey

I really want to see if Cassidy can go away to my golf tournament this weekend, so I know my best bet is to call her dad. I pull up his contact info, dial him up, and take a deep breath. Mr. Maxwell answers on the third ring.

"Hey, bud" he answered, "I saw it was you."

"You busy, Mr. Maxwell?" I inquired with some trepidation.

"Nah, I just dropped off Charlotte, and now I'm just stuck in traffic. What's up?" he asked somewhat urging me to get to the point.

"Well, uh, I was wondering what you would think about Cassidy going with me, um, to my golf tournament this weekend in Asheville. I just really want to hang with her as much as I can before graduation, and I promise it would be totally respectful, um, I just would love for her to be a part of the weekend and see me play" I explained as I fumbled through my words.

"I can see why, she's quite the good luck charm," he said warmly as if to lessen my anxiousness. "I will need to run it by Ashley, and you know she can be a hard nut to crack, but I don't see a problem with it. Trey, I don't see a problem with it because I trust you with my most precious daughter if you know what I mean."

I knew Mr. Maxwell liked me and trusted me. He told me once that he did think what Cassidy and I had was different than other high school relationships. I could see being a part of Cassidy's family. I do believe that some people just find their soulmate earlier in life. I knew Mrs. Maxwell was not on this same page. From what Cassidy had said, Mrs. Maxwell would keep Cassidy frozen in pigtails if she could.

"Oh, yes, sir, Mr. Maxwell. No worries, my parents would be there, too. I just didn't know how you'd feel about her going out of town with us" I clarified.

"Let me check with Ashley, and get back to you tomorrow. And, good luck on your tournament."

"Thank you, sir. See you tonight?" I asked through a smile.

"I'll try, Bud. Have a good one".

Chapter Twelve—Cassidy

It's hard to believe we're already into the month of April. I've never wished for a school year to go by slowly, but I would slam the brakes on this year if I could. Each day that passed was a reminder that Trey would be graduating soon and leaving Franklin. He would be off to exciting things, and I'd be stuck in Franklin eating Wild Bill's with my folks on Wednesdays and missing my best friend, dream guy, and love of my life.

Mom and I rode to school together just like we do every other day. As Mom and I pulled into the teacher parking lot, and headed to our usual spot, she grabbed her ID badge and helped me gather all my things. She looked at me for a second, and said, "Cass, have a good day, honey. Meet me in the parking lot after school."

"Ok, Mom," I chimed back to her, "what's on your plate for today?"

"I'm testing in the overflow room today. I've got a few kids who need to test in a small group. I'm really looking forward to counting the ceiling tiles to pass the time," Mom said exasperated.

"Well, I've got PE first thing," I complained, "that has got to be the dumbest thing. Who decided to have girls sweat right when they get to school when they've just spent 30 minutes straightening their hair? It's like they purposely want us to look unattractive, so the boys wont' be distracted."

"Hmmm," Mom said jokingly, "I'm sure that is the real reason and it has nothing to do with when the Gym is available."

I looked down at my phone when I heard a text from Trey come through.

"Hey. Your dad seems to be down with us going to Asheville. Try and work on your mom," Trey pressured. I got excited for a minute thinking about going away with Trey for the weekend. I would have to tread very lightly with this one.

"Oh, Mom. Did you know Trey has a golf tournament this weekend in Asheville?" I asked.

"I think I remember him saying something about that," she replied.

"I have always wanted to see him in one of his tournaments. It sure would be great if I was able to go to this one and stay with his family," I hinted.

"Um, don't think so," Mom said shutting me down instantly.

"Mom! You didn't even hear me out. Don't say no yet, you haven't gotten all the details," I pleaded with her.

"Cassidy, you are just barely 16 years old, not a college student. You need to get a little more realistic about your requests. I knew this would happen if you started dating a senior. You two are moving way too fast," Mom jabbed back at me.

"You are impossible! Ugh, I can't believe you. Why don't you want me to be happy?" I furiously answered.

Mom reached over to give me a loving pat on the shoulder, but I walked ahead of her without even saying good-bye. I went inside the school in search of Madison. Madison worked in the Front Office during first period as an Office Aide, so it was easy to find her. She was usually running late, though, which is why she wanted to be an Office Aide in the first place. Somehow, she had the Front Office Staff eating out of the palm of her hand, and they'd overlook her frequent tardies. She would win them over by sharing the school gossip with them. She wouldn't tell them anything really juicy but just enough to keep them feeling like they were in the know. She would tell them which teachers flirted with each other, and things like that. Madison was smart that way—Mom called her street-smart.

As I walked through the front doors, I looked over to my left and caught Aseem out of the corner of my eye. Aseem is hard to miss because he's the only kid at my school that wears something on his head like a turban. It's actually like a top-knot covered in fabric. I waved at him and he looked at me shyly and waved back with a small gesture. It was the kind of wave you give when you're not positive the person is really waving at you and you don't want to go full-out wave in case they were looking at the person behind you. I don't know why he wouldn't know I was waving at him, though, because I do every time I see him. It was one of Mom's many requests of me.

I remember Mom telling me about a new student, Aseem, and how he was having a hard time. She would never give details about the students she worked with, but she would hint at things pretty strongly. I gathered from her guarded comments that Aseem was having difficulty assimilating in Franklin and kids weren't being that friendly to him. As always, Mom would end her stories with a plea asking me to be on the look-out for a certain student, or just be extra-nice to one of her students because you never know what a person is battling outside of school or within themselves. After Mom would tell me these stories, I'd start observing these students closely. I couldn't help myself. It was the mini-counselor in me coming out, I guess, because I'd start worrying about these kids, too, just like Mom.

Aseem was probably the one that stuck with me the most because he was always by himself. I'd see him in the morning by his locker and then again during lunch just hanging out all by himself. I thought about how hard it must be to start a new high school with a noticeable difference that there was no way to hide. Not that he'd even want to hide it, and maybe he didn't even have a choice, but still, that takes some pretty serious guts to do day after day. Every now and then, Aseem would catch me looking at him, or checking up on him, I should say, and we'd make eye contact for a brief moment. During those times,

I'd notice his dark, brown, expressive eyes peering out of the most beautiful, creamy, caramel skin, and I'd wonder what was going on behind those eyes.

After waving at Aseem this morning, I kept moving to the Front Office, and noticed Miss Madison had yet to grace us with her presence even though the bell was about to ring. I rushed to my locker to find a tall, handsome guy standing there waiting for me who just happened to make my heart skip a beat. Trey was waiting for me with a big smile on his face. I ran up to him and gave him a quick peck on the cheek.

"Hey there," Trey beamed, "I'll walk down to the Gym with you before I have to go to class. It's OK if I'm a little late. Senior perk."

I looped my arm in Trey's for just a minute as we walked together. Oh, how I was going to miss this next year. I felt a sharp pain in my gut just thinking about it, and quickly rid my mind of those thoughts. I swore to myself that I wouldn't ruin this last bit of time we had together being worried about being apart.

Trey and I walked down the hall together, not daring to acknowledge we would soon be separated. This moment was pure bliss, so idyllic in its' simplicity. Such an uncomplicated moment, going from class to class at the sound of each bell. School provided such a comfort in this way. Bells rang at the same time each day, down to the minute, familiar faces filled the hallways every day, teachers started each class with a warm up and ended with the daily homework assignment. Routine just feels good; it just feels safe to know what's coming next. But, even when you think you've got it down, and it all figured out, life will undoubtedly throw you a curveball. And when it's headed straight for you, you think, maybe I could have been prepared, maybe the signs were there, but I never took the time to notice.

Chapter Thirteen—Aseem

There she was again... the counselor's daughter. She was one of the few people in the school that gave me a second glance. I was actually used to not being noticed, so it always took me off guard when she waved or said hello to me.

I remember when I first started at Franklin. I had transferred from up North because of problems at school. I hate to say bullying because it sounds so angst-y, but there was really no other word for it. Students were obsessed with my hair, tugging at the topknot, asking me what I had under there, and calling me names, like Aladdin and Bin Laden. Even worse, some students would tell me I looked like a terrorist or even act afraid of me. I tried over and over again to explain that I was a Sikh, but no one got it. Eventually, I got kind of roughed up on the bus, and my parents decided to try a new school.

Roughed up, well, that would actually be quite the understatement. I remember it so well, in a PTSD kind of way. I was never liked or accepted at my old school. I would talk to my parents about it, and while they did have sympathy for me, they would always remind me that many men of faith had not been accepted, but their nobility was worth being ostracized before reaching their greatness. I guess that was easy for them to say since they didn't have to go to school every day, and get called names, their hair pulled, and probably what hurt the most, just be completely alienated. It was obvious I would never fit in, and when you're my age, I think that's just what every kid wants. But, I didn't blame my parents, I tried to take their advice of 'turning the other cheek' and 'winning people over with my character', but it just wasn't working.

The bus was probably the worst because the kids were basically wild as the bus driver focused on just getting 60 kids home alive. That final day on the bus was unlike anything I had ever experienced, and hopefully, something that I would never experience again in my lifetime.

As we all crammed on the bus, I went to my usual seat in the back of the bus where I sat by myself. Eighth graders sat in the back, but no one wanted to sit with me, and they'd rather sit three to a seat than to sit with me. In front of me, were three, big kids. They had made fun of me before, but today, one of them decided to take it to a whole new level.

"Hey, Aladdin, what's under that scarf on your head?" he asked.

"My name is Aseem," I replied, "and it's my hair." I tried to remain calm but my pulse was quickening, just like it did anytime someone started calling me names.

"No way," he said. "Show me," he demanded reaching for my patka. I leaned as far back as I could and shook my head 'no'

71

vigorously.

"I said, show me," he pulled at the fabric and started trying to unwrap it.

"No, stop," I pleaded, "Don't touch me, please." It hurt when they pulled at me, but I was more afraid of having my hair down. I would never hear the end of it.

"Hold his arms, guys," he commanded of the other two boys. They did so without putting up any resistance to his requests. I looked at them dead in the eyes, trying to use eye contact to beg of them to have compassion. No such luck. As they struggled with me, the main culprit got my patka off, and my waist-length hair came flowing down. They looked at me first in shock, and then broke out in laughter.

"Look, at him, he's got hair like a girl," they joked. "Aladdin, you sure do have some pretty hair."

Tears welled up in my eyes, and I tried to turn my back to them. I hoped and prayed the bus driver would look back at me, but with the three of them up in their seats, and leaning towards me, I was pretty much invisible. Just when I thought things couldn't get any worse, they did.

"Hey, reach into my backpack and grab my scissors," the big jerk said, "I think Aladdin needs a trim."

"No, I begged. It's for my religion. My hair has never been cut," I hoped this would convince them.

"Well, it's about time. Just a trim," he teased. He grabbed the scissors and snipped at me. I leaned back as far as I could and zig zagged trying to avoid the snipping scissors, but in one horrifying moment, he leaned over further, and was able to snip the ends off the right side of my hair. I gasped.

At that moment, the bus screeched to a halt. I thought perhaps I had been seen by the bus driver or another kid had reported something, but no, it was just the bus stop. The three boys looked at each other, realizing it was their stop, and grabbed their backpacks as if nothing had happened. They exited the bus and I sat in my seat scrunched down as far as I could go, crying. How could I face my parents like this?

I had a few more stops until I would be able to exit the bus. I started combing my hair back, and was able to get it pulled into a ponytail, but there was no way I would be able to wrap it back up before getting off the bus. When the bus came to my street, I peered out the window and saw my mother waiting for me like she always did. I had to face her.

I walked off the bus, and ran to her. She looked at me with confusion, knowing I would never purposely have my hair down at school. I just grabbed hold of her and sobbed. She held me for a long time before asking me what happened. I told her some of the story, but I couldn't bring myself to tell her that my hair had been cut. I hid that fact and it wasn't noticeable with my hair pulled back. But, I knew, and that was bad enough. She was horrified by the parts I did tell her, and reassured me that I wouldn't have to go back to that school. So, that's how I ended up at North Franklin High.

When I registered at North Franklin, Mrs. Maxwell met with my family and me to set my schedule. She was nice right away and instead of acting uncertain about us, she acted interested. I remember her saying that she could tell that we were Sikh's and that I would be the only one at the school, but she would love it if I could educate others, including herself, about our religion and our customs.

I was shy about talking about it, but my dad piped right in, explaining that Sikhism is the fifth largest religion in the world, but just not as common in the United States. He always seems particularly proud of this fact. Then, his typical oration began, citing that many assume that Sikhs follow Hinduism or Islam when in actuality Sikhs are an independent religion. He continued with his familiar sermon about the Sikh religion being focused on love, service, and justice. Mrs. Maxwell seemed very engrossed. After we discussed why we transferred to North Franklin and more about our religion, she wanted to know what my interests were and encouraged me to get involved at school, so I could meet some kids. She also told me that I could come back to her if I ever had any trouble with other students, and she would take care of it right away.

I left her office that day feeling hopeful, but within a few days, I was hitting up against some of the very same problems I had at my old school. Students were grabbing at my head, poking it with a pencil, and inquiring as to why I wore my hair like that. When I explained to them that I had never had my hair cut and it was actually my hair under the fabric, they recoiled and looked at me like I was from another species.

After about a week of trying to navigate North Franklin, I was called down to Mrs. Maxwell's office. My heart was pounding because I assumed I was in trouble. Even though counselors always say, you're not in trouble if you get called to the Counseling Office, I wasn't buying it. So, I sheepishly walked in to the office and was greeted by a nice-looking woman with a friendly smile sitting at the front desk.

"Did Mrs. Maxwell call for you?" she checked.

"Yes, ma'am" I replied with a small tremble breaking through in my voice.

"Oh, OK, then you can go on back" she motioned with her head for me to head to the back of the office.

"Aseem, is that you?" Mrs. Maxwell called out from the back office.

"Yes, my teacher told me you called for me" I explained.

"I did. Come on in." Mrs. Maxwell said as she looked me in the eyes as I walked in the doorway.

I entered the room hesitantly and went over to one of the two wingback chairs that were stationed across from her desk. I just stood there in place kind of hovering over one of the chairs, until Mrs. Maxwell gave me a nod that indicated I should sit down because this might be awhile.

"So, Aseem, how are you enjoying it here at North Franklin High

School?" Mrs. Maxwell questioned with a hopeful look.

I didn't have the heart to tell her the kids here sucked as bad as the ones at my last school, so I lied, and said, "Oh, I like it very much. It's a very nice school."

"Great," she said, "I'm so glad to hear that. We are really glad you are here. We have a lot we could learn from you. In fact, I've been doing some research on Sikhism since you enrolled and I find it very fascinating. That is actually one reason I called you in today."

I swallowed hard. I wasn't sure where this was going. I wasn't used to people showing this much interest in me.

"Aseem, as I was reading more about your religion, I uncovered the 5 K's. Can you tell me more about them?"

Ok, so now I can tell she really has been doing her research. I had an idea of where this was going. There is one 'K' in particular that drew a lot of interest, or concern I should say, from people, particularly school people.

"Sure, Mrs. Maxwell, I can explain them to you. Well, the 'K' everyone notices right away is 'Kesh' which is the uncut hair. I've never cut my hair because in our religion we see it as a gift from God not to be altered. Also, it kind of sets us apart from others, so it makes it obvious we are observing Sikh's."

"Oh, how interesting," Mrs. Maxwell said, "and is that why you wear the head garment to keep it out of your face?"

"Yes, and it is customary. It takes me about 30 minutes every morning to get my hair tied up and set for school," I further explained.

"I hope the other students haven't made you feel uncomfortable in any way about it. They can be very curious at times."

"No, ma'am," I lied, "no one has said anything to me. The other K's aren't noticeable so usually if kids can get past the hair, we are good."

"Oh, yes, please keep telling me about the other four, if you don't mind," Mrs. Maxwell prodded gently.

"Well, there is 'Kanga' which is a special comb we keep tucked in the patka, which is my head covering. The Kanga can be used as a comb but it also represents cleanliness."

"I see, but you are right, no one would ever notice it if they weren't looking."

I started again, "the third 'K' is the 'Kara' which is this bracelet I wear. It symbolizes unity because it's circular with no beginning and no end, just like God. It also is like a reminder when you see it to do the right thing."

"I really like that," Mrs. Maxwell said encouragingly, "a lot of our students could benefit from a constant reminder to do the right thing."

I purposely skipped the next 'K' and moved onto the 'Kachera'.

"The fourth 'K' is the 'Kachera' which is a special undergarment we wear," I said and then paused as my face burned with embarrassment, and then restarted, "which encourages modesty."

"Very fascinating," Mrs. Maxwell nodded, "and what is the fifth 'K'?" she asked expectantly.

"Well," I stammered, "the fifth 'K' is called a 'Kirpan', which is a sign of strength and justice." I began feeling very uncomfortable talking about the Kirpan because it's hard for outsiders to understand it in the right way.

"Is it something all Sikh's wear, too, and what exactly is it?" Mrs. Maxwell pressed.

"Well, it's a dagger," I said with unintended dramatic effect. "It's not what you might think, though. It's just a symbol of respect and justice. Originally, Kirpans were carried by Sikh's so that they could defend others. It's supposed to be used only for noble reasons. But, really, it's more symbolic now, or at least to me."

Mrs. Maxwell immediately looked concerned. "Aseem," she paused, "do you carry a dagger on you?"

"No ma'am," I smiled and pulled out the charm dangling from my necklace, "See, my charm is a small dagger to be worn for symbolic reasons."

I quickly noticed Mrs. Maxwell's face lighten up and she said, "That is so good to know, Aseem. We aren't allowed to have weapons on the school campus, so I was a little concerned there for a minute. I love the meaning behind it, though."

I smiled back at her, and asked if she had any other questions.

"I think that's it for now," she reassured, "but, I do mean it, Aseem, I'm here for you if you need anything. Frankin can be a hard place to break into for some new students. Our kids have good hearts, but they've been a little sheltered, and aren't as open to differences at first as I wish they were. They do usually warm right up after a bit, though."

"No, I'm good," I lied, "the kids here have been fine."

"I'm glad to hear it, and thank you so much for educating me. Maybe we could have you speak in your World Geography class at some point. All the major world religions are covered, and you could share the 5 K's with everyone. It really is quite fascinating."

"We'll see," I conceded. I really couldn't see that happening, but appreciated this woman's unwavering positivity.

"Yes, maybe at the end of the year" she continued, "if you are comfortable with it. Now, let me write you a pass so you can get back to class."

I grabbed my pass, said thank you, and off I went. As I walked out of Mrs. Maxwell's office I patted my waistband out of habit. I could feel the familiar hard metal and was instantly soothed. I couldn't expect her to understand, but I did respect her for asking. I remember walking back to class feeling somewhat emboldened because I once again had gotten past the rules without anyone noticing.

Just then the bell rang, and pulled me out of my thoughts and back to the here and now. Things really hadn't gotten any better since that day. I still hadn't made any friends. I had finally come clean to my parents about school. My mom suggested that I try and look for someone else who looked like they needed a friend, too.

I tried taking her advice, and scoping out the lunchroom for other loners. The next day, I scanned the cafeteria for anyone else who sat alone. Most people were at least paired up, if not, sitting with a big group. But, as I looked at the last row, I noticed a gap of empty seats and then a single kid sitting there eating off the school lunch tray all by his lonesome. I made my way over to him.

"Hey, is anyone sitting here?" I asked as I stood next to the seat behind him.

"Nah, it's open," he responded.

"I'm Aseem," I introduced myself.

"Jason," he replied as briefly as possible.

This wasn't going to be easy. This kid didn't seem that interested in talking to anyone. I decided to keep trying.

"I'm pretty new here. How about you?" I inquired.

He looked at me a little taken aback that I was still trying to make conversation with him. "Um, I'm not new," Jason retorted, but then seemed to warm up just a bit, and asked, "how do you like it here in this hellhole?"

"It's not bad," I said trying to remain optimistic.

"Yea, it is. You don't have to lie," Jason responded dryly, "no one who looks like you could possibly enjoy it here with these ignorant imbeciles."

"Some kids have been a little unevolved, let's just say, but honestly, most kids just seem too busy to notice a new kid," I explained.

"Don't bother, these kids are jerks. I should know. They've been tormenting me for years."

This kid had a real chip on his shoulder. I started to regret sitting next to him. He definitely met the criteria of needing a friend, but I don't think he was up for making one. We awkwardly got through lunch with me asking him benign questions, and him countering with a hateful retort. Finally, the bell rang, and we parted ways.

I thought about Jason later, and became determined not to turn out like him. Some kids here had been jerks to me, too, but I wasn't sure they were being mean-spirited as much as just clueless. I thought about Mrs. Maxwell's suggestion about giving a presentation about Sikhism in my Geography class. You know, it wasn't a half-bad idea, or at least worth a try. Maybe if the kids understood why I looked this way, they'd get used to me, and stop treating me differently. Underneath my hair, and my patka was just a kid like them. If they'd only take the time to notice.

Chapter Fourteen—Aseem

Ugh, testing day. I looked down at my pass and walked in the doorway looking a little confused. Right away I noticed this was not a typical classroom. I saw Mrs. Maxwell and felt relieved to see a face that I recognized.

"This is the Overflow Room, isn't it?" I questioned.

"Yes," Mrs. Maxwell confirmed. "you are in the right place."

I looked around the Overflow Room and could tell it was actually an old Teacher Break Room. The old sink was still present along the back wall, and two walk-in supply closets flanked it on each side. The center of the room was tiny but there was enough room for six desks with a tiny aisle separating one set of three from the other. This room had a window that looked out into the teacher parking lot.

"Strange room, huh?" Mrs. Maxwell said lightly, "we're running out of space in the school, so the few kids who didn't get assigned a testing group, test with me in this old break room. I look forward to alternating between counting ceiling tiles and staring out the window to entertain myself."

I smiled back at her, and waited for the next step as she grabbed the testing materials, and pulled out the testing roster. I glanced down to see what names I might recognize, Ansley Berringer, Emily Kingston, and William Thompson. Vaguely knew who they were, but didn't really know any of them. The testing materials had been set out in alphabetical order on the desks leaving an empty desk between each student.

The morning bell rang and we waited for the other students to arrive. The first student to pop in the door was Ansley. Ansley is a cute, blonde ninth grader with a bubbly personality. Now I remembered that I had seen her before, but I was pretty certain she didn't have a clue who I was.

"Hi, Mrs. M.," Ansley said with a friendly smile.

"Hi Ansley, you can go ahead and have a seat where you see your test booklet and answer sheet" Mrs. Maxwell instructed.

"Can't wait," she laughed and they exchanged another smile.

The next student to walk in was Emily. From what I had seen of Emily, she barely spoke on a good day much less on a testing day. I tried to make eye contact with her, and smiled, but my smile was matched with a blank stare and a frown.

"Hi Emily, we'll get started once everyone arrives. Please find the seat that has a test booklet with your name on it," Mrs. Maxwell explained. Emily complied promptly sitting in the front row and staring forward.

We'll get started as soon as William joins us. Does anyone know if William Thompson is here today?"

"I think he's absent," Emily said. "He always misses school."

"Let's wait another minute or two, and if he doesn't show up, we'll get started with the directions."

We waited a little longer. Mrs. Maxwell said she hoped he would show or that would mean she'd be doing a make-up session and be back in this same room tomorrow. Two minutes went by and then a third and fourth without a sign of William. She finally had to give up hope and assume he was out.

"OK, looks like we can get started now," she confirmed. "Please clear your desk of any items other than your test booklet, answer sheet, and two pencils. Please open your test booklet and read along with me as I read over the directions."

We all diligently opened their booklets and awaited her spiel. I think we could all recite it by now. "You have ninety minutes to take the test, you can't move ahead into another section, you may not use any technology, blah, blah, blah." As she got through the endless list of all the things we may not do, she finally got to the sentence we'd been waiting to hear, "You may begin."

Ansley, Emily, and myself were methodically ticking off questions one by one as Mrs. Maxwell started cruising the room. It looked like she took these opportunities to get in extra steps on her fitness monitor as she paced the floor. A few times I caught her in what looked to be a daydream as she stared intently outside of the window. From the outside of the school, she probably looked like an animal in the zoo stuck behind the glass wall peering out with an unspoken plea to be free.

Especially today, it looked beautiful outside. It was a bright, sunny day with a slight breeze which I could tell from the tree limbs bending faintly in the wind. You could see the leaves rustling in the trees and I sat there for a minute thinking about the sound of those leaves crackling. I also thought about what it would feel like to have the sun on my shoulders. I looked over at Mrs. Maxwell, and she was staring outside intently.

Mrs. Maxwell scanned the room repetitively and made sure that our threesome was moving right along. She circled us again and again making sure we were all marking our answers in the right spaces. Twenty minutes finally passed, and we had a mere seventy more to go. Again, I looked outside and searched for something interesting to daydream about and help pass the time. That's when I saw him.

I saw a figure who looked like a man, but more like a teen, walking through the teacher parking lot. It was hard to make him out completely, but I noticed he had a backpack on and was carrying something in his hand. I squinted so I could try and make out what he held in his hands, but it was still a bit blurry to me. I waited for him to get closer. I started wondering why someone would be in our parking lot in the middle of the day. Maybe it's a workman, I thought. Still, all visitors had to enter through the front office not this back door. As he got closer, I noticed he was wearing a ball-cap, blue jeans, and a black T-shirt with a graphic design on it. It looked like a faded-out lightning bolt which was purposely made to look vintage. Finally, he was close enough that I could get a clear view, and that's when I saw it. My heart rate soared and I could feel it pounding harder and harder as if it might thump right out of my chest. I was gasping for air, but I couldn't get a full breath; it was as if the wind had been knocked out of me. My legs felt heavy as if they were made of lead, and impossible to move. It was like they'd been bolted to the ground. I was frozen.

Did I see what I thought I saw? Was it real? I focused in on his hands again, and my fears were confirmed. He had a gun. He had a gun, and was walking towards the school. I looked up at Mrs. Maxwell in terror, but she must have already seen him. She had already darted to the phone. Mrs. Maxwell quickly dialed 'o' and was able to eek out the words 'Code Red' right before a shot was fired through the door allowing entrance to our school. Before today, North Franklin High was a safe little school where nothing like this was ever supposed to happen.

Chapter Fifteen—Code Red

Wheee-ooo, Wheeee-ooo, Wheeee-ooo. The siren blared throughout the school and throughout the community. This siren sounded like no other alarm heard in the school before. It was apparent this was not a drill. Almost immediately, the sound of doors slamming, feet rushing, and students scrambling, could be heard. I looked around the Overflow Room, and my kids were in disbelief.

Ansley immediately started hyperventilating and had a wild-eyed stare. I could tell she was in complete shock. Emily began to wail from sheer panic with a steady stream of tears trickling down her face. And, Aseem remained stoic, but was trembling as he looked at me with eyes that were pleading to be told what to do next.

I, myself, was in shock momentarily. It took me a second to register what had just occurred. Once it did register, I was briefly transported back to our meeting with Mr. Bagwell. Ok, stay calm. Panicking won't help, and could actually get us all killed.

"Think, Ashley, think," I said to myself. "Oh, yeah, the door, first thing is locking the door," I thought. I ran over to the door, and searched the handle for the lock button, but was quickly reminded that we were not in a classroom, but instead, we were in the old break room, and the door didn't lock. That was it, we were sitting ducks.

"Ok, everyone. We cannot panic. We will follow the protocol and wait for the safety team to arrive. We need to find a place to hide." I ordered.

Just as I gave the order, Emily began wailing again and crying for her mother. Her wails sent my motherly instinct into high gear. I thought of Cassidy and where she might be. Was she safe? Was she somewhere crying for me? I comforted Emily as I scanned the room for the best place for us to hide.

"Kids, kids, pay attention. We are lucky because we have these storage cabinets in the back of the room. I think you all can fit in and no one will know you are here," I directed. We scurried to the back of the room. I had to drag Emily by the arm because she had regressed into a near infantile state and was rendered helpless and unable to function. When I touched her arm she responded with a small whimper like an injured animal.

Aseem and Ansley followed my lead and headed toward the back of the room. We opened the cabinet doors and I could tell we could get Ansley and Emily in one cabinet if they scrunched together, and Aseem in the other one. I quickly pushed them in and gave further directions.

"Listen, we are going to be OK, but you have to promise me you will stay put. You will not come out until you get the all clear, OK? And this is very important, you have to be completely silent. Do you understand?" I said pleadingly.

They nodded except for Emily who just stared blankly. She had quit wailing and had just started rocking herself gently back and forth. Ansley touched her back to comfort her, but Emily did not respond. Aseem stayed surprisingly composed as he slid even further back into the cabinet once used for hanging coats, and now serving as a pseudo-panic room. I closed the cabinet doors and went to begin barricading the door using the desks. But, then I heard it.

Another shot rang through the hallway, and then another in rapid succession. I stood for a minute paralyzed with fear. I grabbed my phone and the walkie we used as administrators to communicate with each other the building. Now, at least, I could connect with the outside world. I crouched down in the front of the room, so as not to give away the location of the students just in case our room was the next point of entry. I typed a quick text message to Nate.

"Shooter at our school. Try to reach Cassidy. I love you."

I could only imagine what must be going through Nate's mind right now. This had always been a distant fear of his. I remember his words clearly, always warning me to lock myself in a room if there was ever an intruder. He told me to look out for myself and make sure that no matter what I could make it home again. Nate would die if he knew I was stuck in a room with an unlocked door very close to a shooter where bullets had already been fired.

I began praying.

"Dear Lord, please keep us safe today. Please change the shooter's heart and provide us with your protection. Lord, please give me the strength I need to get us out of here alive. Amen."

Chapter Sixteen—Code Red (North Franklin Elementary)

"Dear God, please keep everyone at North Franklin High safe," Charlotte's teacher, Ms. Gables, prayed to herself. An email had been sent out by the school principal at North Franklin Elementary briefly informing the staff that the high school was under a Code Red, and the Elementary would go into a Code Yellow out of precaution.

The news of the actual threat spread quickly throughout the school. North Franklin High had an active shooter. Ms. Butler from the room next door burst into Ms. Gables' room and blurted out, "There is a shooter at the high school... an active one, and they haven't found him yet. It's already being reported on the news." She had friends who worked at the high school and was beside herself. Ms. Gables nodded but reminded her that there were little ears nearby.

The protocol was quickly being put in place. The secretary of North Franklin Elementary had come over the intercom announcing we would be in a Code Yellow at this time. Whenever a nearby school was in a lockdown the feeder schools followed suit in the rare possibility that a multiple shooter/multiple location attack was underway. The teachers began trying to calm the fears of the elementary kids.

"Children, we are having a lockdown drill at this time. Remember, what we do in a Code Yellow, right?" Ms. Gables said. The children nodded and began making their way to the back of the room. Ms. Gables turned off the lights and covered the window on the door with black paper. She opened the storage closet in the back of the room. She scurried everyone in the closet and they huddled together and sat down quietly. Some students look concerned, but most were oblivious. Ms. Gables grabbed her class roster and started going through the names of each classmate. Halfway through the list, there was need for pause, then concern, then alarm.

"Charlotte Maxwell," Ms. Gables repeated, "Charlotte Maxwell, please respond." As Ms. Gables scanned the group of kids, she confirmed that Charlotte was not with them.

Ms. Gables stepped back out of the closet and into the dark, classroom. She scanned the room row by row. There, sitting under a desk, holding her knees, and burying her head, was Charlotte. Ms. Gables walked over to her and knelt down beside her.

"Honey, why are you out here?" Ms. Gables asked. She still received no response. She gently put her hand up to Charlotte's face and brushed Charlotte's dark hair off her face, and tucked it behind her ear. "Sweetheart, are you OK?"

Charlotte looked up, but couldn't utter a word. She was shaking slightly and tears were welling up in her eyes. Ms. Gables was at a loss. She kindly put an arm around Charlotte, and pulled her gently to her feet. Charlotte stood up and started to head in the direction of the closet. Once in there, she crawled to the very back and balled up again. This time, she began quivering from head to toe.

It finally dawned on Ms. Gables, and it all made sense. Charlotte's whole world was at North Franklin High. Ms. Gables finished the roll call, and then opted not to sit in the front of the closet where there was more space and a little breathing room. She, too, crawled back to the far corner next to Charlotte and pulled her onto her lap. She began stroking her hair, and gently rocking her. Ms. Gables eyes welled up with tears, too. She thought to herself about the panic that must be in everyone's minds over there. The kids, the teachers, and the parents who were stuck on the outside—helpless.

Chapter Seventeen—Trey (on the outside)

Outside of the school building, it looked like a war zone. Students were filing out of the Gym doors and a few parents had arrived. There was hugging, crying, screaming and that was just the parents. Students were looking around for their friends, texting desperately trying to confirm that their boyfriends, girlfriends, and teammates were safe. I thought I saw a familiar face coming towards me.

It was Cassidy's dad, Mr. Maxwell, running towards me like a bullet heading towards a distant bullseye. He weaved through the people as if on autopilot stepping out of the way here, and slipping to the side to make my way through there. As he reached me, I heard him yell out my name.

"Trey!" he screamed.

"You're here," I responded. "I can't believe this! I was one of the first ones out. I was still in the hallway when the alarm sounded. I had just walked Cassidy into the Gym and was walking back to class. God, I can't believe this! She should be coming out any

95

minute."

"Have they caught him?" Mr. Maxwell asked.

"No, they're just letting the Gym evacuate because they know he entered through the East entrance. From the cameras, I guess. Too far away to get to us before we could get out" I explained. As soon as I said it, I remembered Mrs. Maxwell worked in the East wing.

"He entered through the East entrance? Oh God, that is where Ashley is" Mr. Maxwell sounded panicked. "I came as fast as I could, I knew Ashley would want me to make sure Cassidy made it out OK. Cassidy is her life. I have to be able to send her a text letting her know Cassidy was safe. No matter what I want her to know that," he said sounding choked up. "I have to give her some peace, no matter what," he said as he swallowed hard.

I could tell he had let the unthinkable enter his mind. The thought that Mrs. Maxwell wouldn't be coming out was too hard to think about right now. Cassidy would be devastated. In my head, I scolded myself for even going there in my mind, and regained my wits.

We became laser focused as we watched the door for all the students in the Gym to come out. Finally, I saw the top of Cassidy's head about 50 feet from the door. I stared intently at her so I wouldn't risk losing her for even a second. I felt as if I was willing her to take each step, closer and closer. She was close enough now to see her face. The look of anguish on her face broke my heart. She looked up and our eyes met. I saw a look of relief wash over her face. There was my girl. Thank God. Tears rushed to the corners of my eyes.

Her dad saw her, too, and begin jumping up and down.

"Mr. Maxwell, there she is! Do you see her? She's OK, she's OK. She's going to make it out" I shouted.

My face lit up as a huge smile spread across my face involuntarily. For a moment, I had been relieved of unbearable anguish. But, all of a sudden Cassidy appeared to stop dead in her tracks.

"What the hell is going on?" I said. "Why is she stopping?" I screamed, "Cassidy, come on, Baby. Hurry, hurry now, come on out."

Mr. Maxwell started chiming in, too. "Cass, get out of there. I'm here waiting for you. Please, please, please come out."

Then, the inconceivable happened. Cassidy's face turned to a look of pure horror. She started taking small steps backward looking into our eyes all the while. She took one more small step backward, and then turned around and began running in the opposite direction.

I tried to run in after her, but was immediately stopped by police officers. They held me so tight and looked at me like I was crazy. I'm sure they thought I must be mental to try and run into the line of fire. I struggled to get free from their hold.

Mr. Maxwell came to my rescue and told the officers he was

with me. "Officers, officers, I've got him. I will keep him back."

I was still struggling with all my might. Mr. Maxwell told me he had a feeling that he knew what was going on. He leaned in and told me quietly what he thought had just happened, and then, I let out a scream from the bottom of my gut, "NOOOOOOOO!"

Chapter Eighteen—Cassidy

I had just walked in the Gym when the alarm went off. It took a second for us all to realize that this was not a drill and this siren was unlike any that we'd ever heard. At that moment of realization, it became total chaos. Just as I suspected, no one remains calm in these moments. That's always the first thing they teach you in all of the training—remain calm. The coaches tried to regain control. They were shushing us and telling us to have a seat.

I followed the herd, at first, but then sat down on the bleachers like I was instructed. Not surprisingly, I realized I was a rule follower even in moments of life and death. I sat there thinking for a minute about what could be going on. Had an angry parent entered the building? Had someone accidentally pushed the panic button? I was hoping against all hope that this was the case. The coaches had finally gotten us all quiet, but I knew some kids had already slipped out of the building as the instinct for self-preservation had taken over. The coach's faces looked panic-stricken. There went my hope of a false alarm. I thought about Trey for a second, and prayed he had gotten out of the building and would be there waiting for me.

After a minute or two which seemed like forever, a call came through for the coaches on their walkie telling them to exit us out the back entrance. Coach Brown blew his whistle and said we would be evacuating the building. It was pretty obvious they were just going to have to get all us kids out of the gym because there's no place big enough for us to hide. Coach Brown said we'd have to leave in an orderly fashion with no pushing, and we'd need to be as quiet as possible.

I looked around the room and saw kids crying. Others were typing away on their phones, texting loved ones undoubtedly. At that time, the coaches opened up the gym doors and ushered us into the hallway. I would call this organized chaos. Students were trying not to push but there was a massive bottle neck at the end of the hallway as they reached the exit. I was stuck for a brief moment and saw a text pop up on my phone from Dad. I couldn't stop and text back, but I wanted to so bad. I couldn't stand the thought of him being worried sick. I looked straight ahead as I waited for the hallway to clear up.

As I peered out the glass pane in the door, I could see a mass of people arriving in the back. There were police cars pulling in, parents walking around pacing and talking on their phones, and kids starting to hug when they realized they'd made it out. I started to look intently for Trey. He had to be out here somewhere.

I thought I saw him making his way to the front of the crowd outside. The guy I was looking at appeared to be about Trey's height and the hair looked to be his color. Yes, it was him, I recognized the shirt he was wearing today. Immediate relief filled my body from head to toe. I stared at him closely, and then noticed he started talking to someone next to him. I looked again carefully and saw that it was Dad. Time to make a beeline for them. I picked up my step a little and stared right at them. Shuffling my feet along with all the others edging closer and closer to the doorway and safety.

Coach Brown walked up right behind me. I could tell it was him because I heard the office call for him on the walkie. He was acting very calm and had completely taken charge of the situation. These moments really do show what people are made of, and he was made of steel.

"Office to PE. PE, pick up if you can" Ms. Wright almost begged from the Front Office.

"Coach Brown here" he responded over the walkie.

"Are you evacuating? What is the status?" Ms. Wright asked, and sounded very official.

"We're exiting now. About 50 more kids to get out of the hallway. Has the shooter been located?" he probed.

Well, there it was. Confirmation that there was a shooter in the building. This was real. Way too real.

"Yes, East Hallway...lone shooter. Signing off" Ms. Wright answered.

And, it hit me. East Hallway! That's where Mom was. She had

to be stuck over there. They wouldn't be evacuating them. What had she told me she would be doing today? Think, Cassidy. Where was she? I started mentally retracing our steps this morning. I was complaining about PE, and she was complaining about something, too. What was it? I remembered. Mom was in the Overflow Room. I had to get there. I hesitated and started to ease backwards.

I looked into Trey's eyes as he looked back at me with confusion. I could melt into those eyes. He was everything to me. I wanted to run into his arms so badly. I wanted to run away with him, far away right now, but I felt an indescribable pull towards my mom. If something ever happened to her, I could never forgive myself for not being there for her. I felt like I needed to protect her. I looked back at Trey once more, and his face looked pitiful as he seemed to be begging me to run to him. I hesitated for a quick second, then took a few steps backwards very slowly, and finally I turned and ran.

Chapter Nineteen—Madison

How did I end up here? I remember getting to school, and going to the Front Office. I grabbed the bucket with the extra pencils and things they'd wanted me to distribute to the teacher's rooms who were testing. As I headed down the hallway, I heard a loud pop. I looked around to see if anyone else heard it, too, but the halls were pretty clear with a few kids scrambling. I guess it made sense that I was a loner out here because I was late after all. At about that same time, the loudest sounding alarm that I'd ever heard of bombarded the building. For a minute, I was confused about where to go. I looked to the side and he was standing right there.

Pop. I was hit. I grabbed my side where the bullet had gone in, and immediately felt the wetness and warmth of blood on my hands. What the hell? Why was someone shooting people at school? I fell to the ground. Did it hurt? Yes, but not like you would think. It was like getting punched in the side. The impact of the bullet tore through my side through skin, muscle, and tissue and it felt like someone had hit me with a bat. Then, it went kind of numb. I laid there still as could be, so the shooter would think I was dead. I hoped that would be the one and only bullet.

I heard his footsteps hurriedly go past me. Thank God, he didn't go in for the kill. I lay there still. I really couldn't move anyway. My thoughts were all over the place. I was thinking about what was going on here. I couldn't see the face of the guy who took a shot at me, but could see from his size and frame that he was probably a teenager. Who would want to do this? Who would want to kill me? What kind of psycho walks into a school and just starts shooting? A coward, that's who! Purposely going where no one can fight back. Why was he here? I don't think he was out to get me as much as I was in the wrong place at the wrong time. Why? Why? Why was I in his path?

I immediately thought of Cassidy. I was late today so we didn't even get to talk this morning. I prayed that she would be safe. And Trey, too, and Mrs. Maxwell. Where are they now? Probably in the Gym far away. They could get away, I bet as long as he's on his own, and there are no other shooters. Mrs. Maxwell could be anywhere. She was always working all over the school. You never knew where she was going to pop up. Please let this end soon, so no one else gets hurt. Please let someone rescue me soon. I've seen enough Crime TV to know that I couldn't just lay here bleeding for too long without bleeding out. It really hit me for a second that this could be it. This could be the end of me. I had so much I had wanted to do in my life, and now I might not have the chance. I had dreams of becoming famous and having my father finally notice me again. I felt tears come to my eyes.

I thought of my mom. I was all she had. I couldn't leave her all alone. Maybe we didn't have a perfect family, but it was a family and I wouldn't have traded her for anything. I thought of how she needs me to help her, remind her of things, just keep her on track, so I tried to force myself to fight for her. I lifted my head just slightly, but I felt so weak. It felt as if my body was encased in concrete. I lowered my head again, and looked to my side. I saw a pool of blood reaching from my side down towards my feet. I felt really tired and I just wanted to close my eyes and pretend that this was a bad dream. As I closed my eyes, I daydreamed about being far away from here. I thought about Cassidy and I going to the beach together. Spending all day in the sun, not wearing enough sunscreen so we could be savage tan, and me getting really dark and her getting burned. I dreamed about us braiding each other's hair and sharing our clothes and make up. I thought about all of our talks about us staying together forever. We planned to be roommates once we graduated from North Franklin. We knew we could get along well because we practically spent every day together for years, and even if we fought, we got over it within a few minutes. I could never stay mad at Cassidy, my sister.

As I thought about Cassidy, I tried to gain some more energy to check out what was going on. I lifted my head one more time, and this time I opened my eyes and peered into the doorway across from me. There, staring right back at me was Mrs. Maxwell. Was I hallucinating? I thought maybe I was but I saw the look on her face and I knew it was real. The look on her face was one of utter terror. I must be worse off than I thought. I gazed at her for a few seconds. I knew there was no way I could get to her, so I gave her a look that I hoped she understood. I looked at her the way a child looks up to their parent. Pure admiration and adoration. I loved her and I wanted her to know.

Chapter Twenty—Mrs. Maxwell

After the first two shots, there was a pause. I was so unprepared. My door wouldn't lock, I didn't have paper to cover the window in my door, and I had kids shoved in cabinets as a safety plan. I thought about Mr. Bagwell's speech again. Lock your door. Impossible. Cover your window. Can't. Barricade your door. OK, this I could do. I started grabbing a desk and pushing it over to block the door. I lifted it so as not to make any noise. As I sat it down quietly by the doorway, curiosity got the best of me, and I peeked out of the window.

I saw the body of a crumpled teen stretched out across the floor. There was a puddle of blood from the waist down seeping into the student's clothes and shoes. It was a girl. My heart ached. Some mother may not have their little girl coming home today and it broke my heart. It looked like a scene from a horror movie out there. I glanced up and down the hallway, and couldn't spot the shooter. I gazed back at the body which appeared to be lifelessly frozen not moving an inch. I examined it more closely. From the feet up, I could see the body was slight. She had flats on her feet which led up to her dark, blue jeans, and then an untucked, blue and white plaid flannel shirt. Once my inspection reached her shoulders, I noticed her hair. Could it really be her? I would recognize that dark, wavy hair anywhere. I had seen that hair what seemed like a million times. Then, she turned towards me and our eyes met. It was Madison.

Madison stared at me intently with the most loving eyes. I stared back at her in dismay. I felt as if my own child was out there dying. I had known that little girl her whole life and to see her like this was excruciating. I remembered what Mr. Bagwell said about not opening a locked door. My door wasn't locked but if I went out into the hallway, the shooter might see me, and worse, might enter my room and find the other kids. We could all die. I looked back at Madison but she had already laid her head back down. My eyes veered back to the blood surrounding Madison's body and I knew she wouldn't make it much longer. I had to be there for her. I could try to get help for her. And as I took a deep gulp, I acknowledged an even worse thought. I couldn't let her die alone.

I creaked open the door as quietly as possible. Looking to my left and to my right, I could see that the coast was clear, at least for the moment. I tiptoed across the hallway with my heart pounding like a ticking bomb. I put my hand on Madison's shoulder, and she raised her head just slightly. She gave me a look and then the smallest of smiles.

"Madison, we have to move you very quietly. I'm going to need to drag you into the Overflow Room. I know it might hurt, sweetie, but you've got to be very quiet" I coached. Madison didn't respond.

I reached my arms under her armpits and got a grip on Madison

107

and began to pull her. She was about 120 pounds, so I couldn't just hoist her on my back. I began to drag her across the floor.

"Uhhhhhh," Madison groaned.

"Shhhh, sweetheart. We're almost there."

We entered the doorway and I pulled Madison inside. I positioned Madison towards the back of the room near the sink. I went back to ensure the door was closed completely and saw something horrifying. There was a trail of blood leading straight into our room. There was no question where we were hiding. There was also no question that someone else had dragged Madison in here. I couldn't do anything about this now. Truth is, I wouldn't have made another decision. Madison was like my own. I owed it to her to be with her now. I owed it to her mother to stand-in for her as Madison was at her weakest point.

I went back to Madison's side and grabbed some paper towels from the sink. I bunched several of them together and placed them on Madison's side and applied pressure. I tried to soothe Madison by talking to her.

"Maddie, I'm here now, and everything is going to be alright," I said fairly convincingly even though I wasn't even convinced of that myself.

"Am I dying?" Madison uttered.

"No, Madison, you got hit on the side which is probably the best place you can get hit. The doctors will be able to stitch you back up and get you back good as new."

"I love you," Madison said.

"And, I love you," I responded and the tears came flowing down my cheeks. I started stoking Madison's hair and put her head in my lap. I couldn't help but stare directly at her beautiful face. Her tan skin perfectly flawless, her striking eyes closed for now but framed with the darkest, longest eyelashes curled up ever so slightly. I reached down and kissed her on the cheek and whispered, "I love you a bushel and a peck".

I looked down at my phone and wanted to call Nate, but didn't want to take the chance of being heard. I decided to text him again. I looked down at my phone and saw there was a text from him.

"Here now. I'm with Trey. Cassidy is making her way out to us."

Praise God. The enormity of not having to worry about her safety felt like momentary bliss. Anything could happen to me at this point if I knew she was safe. Doesn't every mother feel this way? She was part of me and if she survived, then it was as if I had made it out, too.

I texted Nate, "Keep Cass safe."

Then, I heard it. Steps, steps, coming toward our room. I peeled my cardigan off and laid it under Madison's head. I stood to rush back to the business of barricading the door. As I reached the door, I looked out and screeched, "NOOOOO."

Chapter Twenty-One—Cassidy

I made it out of the West Hallway, running as fast as I could. I quickly scanned the doors I was passing, and each classroom door was closed with a black poster covering the window. I made a left turn, ran past the Media Center, and into the East Hallway through the back entrance. I came up on the Overflow Room, and noticed something slick, and reddish brown smeared across the floor.

There was a line of blood leading up to the door of the Overflow Room. My breathing became heavier and heavier and my pulse raced. Who had been shot? Was mom shot as she made her way down here and then crawled into the room? Was I too late, too late to say goodbye?

I looked in the window of the Overflow Room, and saw her face. She looked back at me and screamed "Noooo" as she focused on my face. I pushed open the door and wrapped my arms around Mom's waist in the tightest embrace. She was here. She was still alive. I cried sobs of relief.

"Cass, why are you here? I thought you were out with Dad and

Trey," Mom questioned incredulously.

"Mom, I couldn't leave you in here. I had to be where you were. I just had to," I explained.

"Oh, Cass," Mom sighed, "I wanted you safe."

At that moment, I looked past Mom and saw someone laying on the ground. I saw the blood all around her. It took me just a second to figure out it was Madison.

"Madison!" I shrieked. "Oh My God, Madison! Mom, what happened?" I cried uncontrollably. "Is she going to die?

Mom stayed calm, and looked at Madison making sure she couldn't see her, then she nodded at me up and down with the saddest expression I had ever seen. How could this be? Of all people, how did Madison get caught up in this bullshit? Madison was adored, how could anyone want to hurt her?

I ran to Madison's side, and started reassuring her. "Hey doll, it's me, Cass," I said as I rubbed her back. "You are going to be OK. Mom and I will make sure of it. You have to, OK? Who else could I tell all my secrets to?"

Madison reached for my hand briefly and squeezed it. Her skin looked pale for her, and her breathing was labored as she took shallow breaths in and out. She dropped my hand gently.

"Madison, I love you," I cried and put my head in her hair. I sobbed as Mom came over to console me. She reached her hand under my chin and lifted it towards her. She wiped the tears from my eyes and kissed my cheek. We hugged each other tight.

"Cass, you are going to need to hide. I will stay out here with Madison," Mom commanded. There is probably room for you in the back cabinet with Aseem. She ran over to the cabinet on the left and flung open the door. There stood Aseem trembling inside.

"Aseem, we are still undiscovered. Keep doing what you are doing. Not a peep. Cassidy is coming in with you," Mom clarified to Aseem who I don't think could make a peep right now if he tried.

"Mom, I don't want to leave you out here. Can't you hide somewhere, too?" I nearly pleaded.

"Honey, you know I can't let Madison be out here all alone. You have to hide, though. I can't take it one more minute knowing that you are out here. Go, now," Mom rationalized.

And, I knew it, too. Mom would never leave Madison out there injured and hurting. I squeezed her tight with tears rolling down my face.

"Mom, I love you so much. I know I don't always show it, but I love you more than anything. You have been the best mom anyone could ever ask for," I declared through tears.

"I love you, Cass, a bushel and a peck," she choked out trying not to cry and then she implored, "Do not come out, no matter what you hear. Do you understand? No matter what, stay in here, perfectly silent."

I nodded, and crawled into the cabinet next to Aseem. There wouldn't have been room for Mom in here anyway as we could barely fit. Luckily, we were both on the small side. Aseem stared at me for a moment recognizing me as the girl who always waves at him. I know he wished he had never come to this school. I tried to make eye contact with him, but he just turned his head and began staring forward again. I pressed my ear near the cabinet door, so I might be able to hear what would happen next. Right now, all I could hear was silence. Precious silence.

I thought about Trey and wanted to cry. How safe I would feel in his arms right now. What must he be thinking? And Dad, too? And what about poor Charlotte? I hoped she didn't know what was going on over here.

"God, please, send someone to save us. God, please, please, please, help us. Please don't let the shooter notice us," I begged silently in my prayers.

Chapter Twenty-Two—Intruder

I had planned this day for a while now. I was tired of going unnoticed. At first, I had been noticed, but for all the wrong reasons. I was mocked mercilessly all through middle school. I was known as the bed-wetter, the overweight kid, the kid with acne, you name it, anything bad, I had it. I had like one friend in middle school and he was a bad off as me. We would commiserate together. We railed on the popular kids. We hated them with a passion. I don't know who they thought they were, acting so great because they could go out and spend Daddy's money, and were good athletes.

First, I would try to ignore it when they would call me "Tubby" or "Zit Face", but then it became a daily thing. Ignoring didn't help at all. I thought about telling my parents, but I didn't want them to see me as pitiful. So, I just acted like it didn't bother me. They all thought I was shy, but really I was just fuming on the inside.

I guess maturity caught up with these kids a little bit because in high school they started to lay off. But, then it wasn't like they started being nice to me or calling me by my real name, they just stopped calling me by anything at all. It was like I didn't even exist. I would see them high-fiving each other in the hallway, and saving each other seats in the cafeteria, and dating all the hot girls, and it made me seethe. These guys were total dumbasses and wouldn't amount to anything in the real world, but here it was like they were the kings of the kingdom and everyone else bowed down to them. Everyone looked up to the popular kids—their skin was clear, their hair was perfect, they dressed perfectly like they were models wearing all the latest trends. There were girls in my school who I swear never did wear the same thing twice. Idiots trying to look like individuals, but actually little clones of each other.

There was one kid in particular who drove me crazy, Bryan Pope. He had been the biggest instigator in middle school. He was the kind of kid who got away with a lot just because everyone else was afraid to piss him off. It was like as long as the spotlight of teasing was on me and a few others, then they were safe, so they chimed in, too, almost as a defense mechanism. I hated them, too, but not as much, because I couldn't be sure I wouldn't do the same thing if I had been in their shoes.

As for Bryan, it was just what you would expect. Tall for his age, good looking, according to the girls, and a great baseball player. He was oohed and ahhed over by all the coaches. It all went to his head and made him an even bigger monster. He thought he was invincible. Sometimes, he would just walk by me and thump me on the head. It wouldn't even be to show off for some other kids because sometimes no one was even watching, it was just because he could. He wanted to establish the pecking order—Ok, ok, we got it, you and your type are at the top and we're at the bottom. For now!

So, I carried a lot of anger toward this kid. You can imagine after years of this torture, it wasn't like I could just let it go. I was like a pressure cooker ready to blow. So, this year, much to my distaste, Bryan showed up in my Math class. He sat with the most popular girl in our grade, Lauren. She was actually pretty nice, and would say hi to me and actually call me by name, Jason. Maybe it's true that girls mature faster than boys. She was mature in all the right places, if you know what I mean. And beautiful, too. Lauren had long, dark brown hair and dark brown eyes to match. She had the nicest smile, and would willingly give it out freely.

As soon as Bryan would come in, though, all bets were off. He was so loud that there was no way to tune him out. Isn't that always the way, the biggest jerks talk about 100 decibels above everyone else. They aren't happy unless they can hear themselves above all else. So, as much as I might have liked to ignore this POS, I couldn't. He would say all kinds of rude things to Lauren. Like really sexual things. She would just tell him to stop it, but would kind of awkwardly laugh afterwards.

I couldn't take it anymore, so I fired back at him to "Shut up and leave her alone." He started cackling at me. I remember it vividly.

"Lauren, get a load of this guy. He thinks he is coming to your rescue. Isn't that sweet? You got a new boyfriend?" Bryan mocked.

"Bryan, just leave it alone, please," Lauren appealed to him.

"No, he's so cool. He's like your knight in shining armor. You got yourself a real winner there, Lauren," Bryan teased cruelly.

I wish I'd had the guts then to just haul off and hit him. But, my face burned red with embarrassment, and I just sat there like a little wimp. Fortunately, the teacher began instruction and the room had to quiet down. Unfortunately, I had earned myself a new nickname, "Hero". Now, I was greeted daily with "Hey, Hero" and "Hero, you got any villains to slay today?" It was stupid, but just rubbed and rubbed on an open wound.

Then, I got myself into some trouble. I wrote about wanting to take down the popular kids in one of my essays in English. I gave a few specifics about how I'd like to shut one of them up permanently. My teacher turned it into the guidance counselor out of concern. And, next thing I knew, I was in Mrs. Maxwell's office.

The events that started that day drove me to make the plan I am carrying out now. I was tired of being invisible and unnoticed by most of the kids at my school. I thought of a way that I would leave a mark on them and no one would forget who I was. They would rue the day they antagonized this guy. We may seem harmless, but we have enough brains and enough torture in our souls, to light up the whole school.

When I came into the school, I knew just where to go. The school was supposed to be secure, but one bullet would take care of that obstacle. I knew the back door to the East Hallway was fairly secluded so I would come in that door and just take a shot at anyone I saw. And, that's exactly what I did. I thought I'd have some time before anyone even noticed me, but somehow the panic button was hit right away. Whatever... I could still accomplish what I started out to do, and I knew I wasn't going to make it out of here alive. It was a big price to pay for a worthwhile legacy, but one that I was willing to pay for infamy.

When I shot the door, kids must have scattered everywhere. I ran in, but doors were being slammed and I became a little disoriented about what to do first. Then, I saw one of the popular girls coming down the hallway and I took my shot. She fell to the ground immediately. She didn't even know what or who hit her. One down. I kept moving down the hallway towards the Media Center. These kids had moved fast because there was no one left just stuck out in the hallways. I thought I'd go back and see what was going on with the girl I shot. Someone was probably out there trying to help her.

I looked down the hallway and picked up my step. Her body was gone. I couldn't believe she'd been able to get up and move. But then, I noticed drag marks in blood leading from where she'd been hit to the room directly across the hallway. Aha—there had to be others inside. Bingo. I put my hand on the door and opened it. Not locked—fools.

There she was, the girl I hit, laying on the ground still covered in blood. Right next to her, kind of leaning over her was a familiar face looking straight back at me. Her eyes were fixed on me and she looked like a deer caught in headlights. She was finally able to muster out a word.

"You?" she said.

Chapter Twenty-Three—Mrs. Maxwell

It was him. Jason Marshall. Jason Marshall, a killer? I knew Jason. I had actually felt sorry for him, but he had been that kid who I just couldn't get an accurate read on. My read was more dark-loner, not murderous assassin.

Jason first came to my attention when Ms. Thompson emailed me to tell me about something he had written in his paper, Life's Lessons. The paper was intended to be a reflection piece about different moments in the student's life that had occurred and then imparted a lesson that stuck. Most students wrote about a death in the family, something hard that they'd had to overcome, maybe a phobia that they had conquered or dealing with a big disappointment that turned into a positive growth experience. Sometimes this particular assignment would dredge up something alarming, and a teacher would hustle down to my office to get my opinion on the situation.

When Ms. Thompson emailed me, she was vague. It was obvious in her tone, though, that we'd need to get together right away. I was never sure if there was going to be a real cause for concern or not, but the teachers were on such high alarm
out of fear of doing the wrong thing, that we took everything

seriously.

"Alert. Alert. Life's Lessons strikes again. This one needs immediate attention. Are you around?" Ms. Thompson questioned in her email.

"Hey. I'm here. Can you come down to my office?" I responded.

"Be there in five," she confirmed.

True to her word, Ms. Thompson came bounding in my office within five minutes. She was a little out of breath as she stood in the doorway with a cluster of paper in her hands. Her usual smile was missing, and a concerned look was spread across her face.

"Hey, OK, take a look at this. His life lessons are all about being bullied. But instead of saying the typical "what doesn't kill you makes you stronger", his lesson learned was "the weak shall overcome." And by overcome, he means obliterate. Take a look at this paragraph," she requested.

I took a look at the paper, and began reading Jason's rant. It began innocently enough, but quickly turned dark. Every now and then, a student does or says something that feels so ominous, I feel compelled to act urgently. This was one of those times.

The excerpt that struck me as particularly threatening was the third paragraph down. In it, Jason wrote, "life has taught me that no one looks out for the little guy. The little guy is ridiculed, harassed, and mocked. With each taunt, the little guy becomes smaller and smaller until he's almost invisible. He's so small, and so unnoticed that he can do things without being seen. He starts making plans to even the score. He has a target that has picked at him over the years like some pick at their scabs. Pick, pick, pick, opening the wound again until it feels freshly injured. But the little guy, takes his time, and plots his revenge. He will turn the tables. When the target least expects it, the small and invisible infiltrate. They can silence the loud-mouths, all it takes is a pistol and a little ammo. Open wide, loud mouth. So, there it is, my life lesson, "the weak shall overcome."

"This is very disturbing," I commented in disbelief. "I'm going to speak to him right away. I will need to do a threat assessment, too. Thank you for letting me know. You, teachers, are the eyes and ears of the school, you truly are."

"It just really, really gave me the creeps. Actually, this Jason kid gives me the creeps anyway," Ms. Thompson said as she scrunched up her shoulders and imitated a lengthy quiver. "He is a loner and never smiles, come to think of it, I don't think I've ever seen him talking with any friends."

"I'll let you know what I find out," I reassured her. As Ms. Thompson left, I checked the scheduling system, so I could pull up Jason's schedule. He was in third period with Coach Brown this period, so I grabbed the walkie and called down to the Gym.

"Counseling to PE," I called out over the walkie.

"PE, here," Coach Brown responded.

"Coach, can you send Jason Marshall to the Counseling Office, please."

"You got it. He's on his way."

Within a few minutes, Jason stood at my door. He was pasty, white, with dark, oily hair and a face full of pimples. I felt sorry for him immediately as I knew it's not easy to go through high school with acne. I motioned for Jason to have a seat.

"Jason, I called you to my office today because of some things you wrote in your English paper," I explained cutting right to the chase. "Things that were very dark, and frankly, quite disturbing."

"Oh, I think I know what you are talking about," he said.

"Really? What do you think I'm referring to?" I pressed.

"Just the stuff I wrote about revenge," he replied almost non-chalantly.

"Well, you would be right about that. You were pretty specific about wanting to shut some people up," I continued to push.

"Nah, that was just for the assignment. You know, trying to be dramatic, or impactful as my Lit teacher would say," Jason smoothly put the ball back in my court.

"Jason, what you wrote really concerned me. I think there must have been some truth to what you said. It was very convincing. And, even if you didn't mean it, there are some things you just do not say in school papers. You do realize we are living in dangerous times, and all threats or threatening comments are taken very seriously," I warned.

"I'm fully aware that the school tends to overblow things, yes. But no, I don't have a vendetta against anyone. And, I don't plan to take revenge on anyone if that's what you are worried about," he responded with irritation at this point.

"We haven't had a reason to meet before today, so I'm just trying to get to know where you are coming from a little better. Is that OK?" I pursued.

"Sure, what do you want to know? I'm an open book," he declared with sarcasm dripping from his words.

"Well, what do you like to do at school? Any clubs? Sports?" I inquired. I was checking for any connections at school known as protective factors for students. If students were connected at school, there was a much less likely chance they would put themselves or others at risk.

"Nope," Jason exclaimed glaring at me.

"How about friends, who are some of your friends at school?" I probed again.

"Let's see, there are too many to count," Jason answered and then countered, "Who are some of your friends?"

I could feel my blood beginning to boil.

"Ok, Jason, here's the deal. What you wrote could be considered a threat. Threats are taken seriously. We do an assessment to see if you are a danger which involves interviewing you, and calling your parents to see if you have access to any items that could be dangerous," I said with a no-nonsense tone. I hoped to get my point across that we were no longer playing games.

"Jason, based on our interview, I'm not convinced that you weren't serious about what you wrote in your paper. I'm going to call home now, and speak with your parents," I disclosed. And then, I saw a look come over Jason's face of utter furor.

"Why don't you spend your time trying to track down the kids that make my life hell instead of picking on me?" Jason retorted.

"Jason, I will be happy to look into that, too. But, you have to report these things to me. I can't help you if you don't tell me what's going on" I softened.

"Not interested," he answered defiantly.

At that moment, I looked at Jason, and I felt for him. It's very much counselor-speak, but I thought about the adage, "hurt people, hurt people", and I could see the hurt in Jason almost pouring over.

"That's your choice, Jason, but I do want you to know I'm here for you. If someone is mistreating you, I want to know about it. If you don't feel comfortable talking about it, you can write me a note," I encouraged. "I do need to call your parents and tell them about our discussion. Not because I'm trying to get you into trouble, but because I'm still worried about what you wrote and the level of anger you seem to have. I can give your parents some resources that might be helpful and can suggest that you spend some time talking with a counselor about these feelings that you have."

Jason looked at me as if he was pondering opening up to me. But, stopped himself, and asked if he could go back to class. I gave him a pass, and followed up with a phone call to his mother. She answered the phone quickly and listened thoroughly to what I told her. She assured me that Jason didn't have access to any weapons, and just had a flair for the dramatic. I told Mrs. Marshall that I thought Jason could benefit from some counseling, and told her that I would be sending her a list of recommended professionals. Mrs. Marshall agreed to look them over, but it seemed more to appease me than anything else.

After hanging up with Mrs. Marshall, I felt torn. Jason hadn't made a direct threat against anyone by name. When questioned, he denied it, and his mother was informed. I knew I had followed the standard procedure, but I was still distressed about our interaction. I put a note on my calendar to follow up with Jason in one week. Like it or not, he was going to be seeing more of me.

Not even a week had past, and I was seeing Jason again in my office. This time, a distressed parent had contacted me over email with concerns about school safety. Jason had posted some things online that had alerted him and he wanted to make a report to the school right away. I wrote them back telling them that I was free later around 10:00 AM that day, if they wanted to come in for a discussion.

At 9:57 AM, Mr. Barrios showed up in the Counseling Office. He wore a serious look on his face, and carried a handful of papers with him. I told him to please step into my office, so we could discuss his concerns.

"Mrs. Maxwell, one of your students, is posting threats against the students in the school online. Many people have seen these posts and are very concerned about this student's well-being and his mental stability to be honest."

"Can you please tell me more about the specific comments?' I inquired.

"Yes, I've screenshotted some of the worst ones so you can see for yourself."

I looked through papers and immediately knew why so many parents were worried. The first posts were directed at the "suck up's" asking why so many kids at North Franklin were like sheep following around Bryan Pope and his friends. He criticized their lack of originality, lack of backbone, and lack of integrity. The last comment was the clincher, "little sheep flock together, but little do they know, they are being led to the slaughter." This kid was scary, he really was.

But, it didn't stop there. The next posts were directed to Bryan himself. It read, "Bryan Pope, high on dope, was found hanging from a rope. And, all the little people of North Franklin gathered to mourn, and what happened next made them wish they'd never been born." This post in itself left us with no other choice, but to do what we did, suspend Jason Marshall. And, unbeknownst to us, we were setting off a chain of events that once started was irreversible.

After reassuring Mr. Barrios that the matter would be dealt with swiftly and severely, I ran to our principal, Mr. Johnson's office. I relayed the message to him and he agreed, based on this incident along with the English paper, we had no choice but to suspend him and recommend that his parents take him for a psychiatric evaluation.

I called Mr. and Mrs. Marshall and asked them to come to the school immediately. They arrived and I told them what had been reported. The only word I could use to describe their reaction was 'denial'. They immediately stepped in with the excuses. "Jason is into creative writing," they rationalized. "Jason wouldn't hurt a flea, he just likes to say things for shock value," they justified. Finally, I had to tell them that these were considered threats and he was given out of school suspension for ten days. I strongly recommended a psychiatric evaluation, unfortunately, I knew the school system was not allowed to require one. Mr. Marshall looked at me like I was the one who needed my head examined. "We'll see," he scoffed. Finally, we called Jason down to tell him the news.

As Jason edged towards my office, he noticed that not one but both of his parents sat in the two wingback chairs across from my desk. "So, let me guess, you all are freaking out about what I posted online last night, right?" Jason asked.

"Yes, Jason, you have quite a few people concerned about these consistently dark, threatening messages you keep putting out there." I confirmed.

"First of all, none of this happened at school so there's nothing the school can do about it. Secondly, I didn't mean it as a threat, just trying to express myself," Jason excused while giving his parents a distressed look.

"Actually, the school can assign consequences when your off-campus behavior affects the students within our building. You can read about it in the Student Code of Conduct, under disruption of a public school. Do you really think that the students you targeted can focus on learning today?" I clarified with a notably angry tone.

"This is bogus. Mom, Dad, you know these kids have been cruel to me for years. And, now, they're going to act scared of me. Give me a break," Jason balked.

"Listen, Jason, it seems like you've got a lot of built up hostility towards several students in the building. I do understand that, and part of me, is glad you've finally found your voice. But, you are not using it in the right way. It is one thing to defend yourself and another thing entirely to become the aggressor. That's where we stand now, with you as the aggressor. And, Jason, we are left with no choice, but to suspend you for ten days. After ten days, you may return, but any similar incidence in the future, will be cause for dismissal from our building permanently." I said as clearly and definitively as I could.

Jason couldn't believe what he was hearing. He glared at me with detest. He stood up right then and there and walked straight out the door with his parents following closely after him.

I planned to follow up with Jason when he returned, but I didn't expect to see him for several days. Startlingly, it was only a matter of days before I would be seeing him again. This time we were meeting not as student and counselor, but as predator and prey. He would unexpectedly end up threatening not only my life, but also the life of my students, and my own precious daughter.

When I realized it was Jason at the door and that he was the intruder. I felt I had to try and talk some sense into him. Maybe I could reach him, I thought idealistically.

"Yes, it's me," Jason replied. He pointed the gun towards me. He aimed right at me from just a few feet away.

"Jason, wait, wait, I know you think you have to go through with this, but you don't. You could still walk out of here with me. I would tell them not to shoot, and let them know that you showed me mercy. You wouldn't be in that much trouble. I would testify for you, I promise," I begged.

Jason stared at me. He looked deep into my eyes, and continued to edge closer to me. Again, he pointed the gun at me.

"Well, I wasn't expecting to see you in here," Jason declared, "it's nothing personal by the way, but I'm going to finish what I started."

"But, Jason, why? Shooting me won't prove anything. I know you've been through a lot and no one blames you for being angry. But, I promise, I'm not the enemy. I can be your ally. Just trust me. Let's walk out of here together," I urged. I was thinking of stalling him until the officers could intervene.

"No one cared about me before, but now, they'll be sorry. April 9th will never pass again in Franklin without people thinking about me and what I did. They'll remember Jason Marshall," he bragged.

I kept stepping back further and further, stalling him. But then, I could tell by the look on his face, that he was growing weary of my pleas.

"Don't move," Jason shouted.

He aimed the gun straight at my chest, and I could sense this was it. I had nothing to lose, so I lunged at him, and shockingly was able to knock the gun from his hands. It spun around as it hit the floor and settled into a resting spot under the desk nearby. We both dove for the gun and I fought tooth and nail to hold his hand back away from the gun. The room was loud with the sounds of scuffling. I silently prayed for Cassidy and the other kids to stay put.

Finally, Jason got his hand on the butt of the gun, and was able to tighten his grip around it. This was it. I braced myself for the inevitable. Thoughts of Charlotte raced through my mind. How I wanted to be able to see her toothy grin again. The calm of her waving goodbye to me this morning seemed like another world. I closed my eyes tight and tried to transport myself to this morning when all was right in the world, and my biggest worry was making it to school on time. Funny how I wanted to make a difference with my life by helping kids, and in the end, I was going to be taken out by one of them.

Chapter Twenty-Four—Aseem

Staying perfectly silent was excruciating. I wanted to cry, but I was too terrified to even muster up tears. I listened closely through the cabinet door. For a brief moment, I felt a small reprieve of the fear of imminent death. There was nothing but the sound of silence for a few minutes, and it was almost calming. For just a moment, I even felt hope sink in, hope that we would be rescued. But, that sense of hope was quickly dashed as a rush of noise came surging in our room. I finally heard his voice.

It wasn't like it thought it would be. It wasn't commanding, or overly masculine. It just sounded like another kid. I heard him talking to someone who had to be Mrs. Maxwell because I had already gathered the other body in the room with them wasn't making a peep. I pleaded with the girls in the other cabinet in my mind, "Please don't give us away. Please don't make a sound."

The counselor's daughter was standing as close to me as humanly possible. We had no choice, we were in a life or death situation and this cabinet was the only thing keeping us alive.

She had her ear pressed to the door, and was straining to hear every footstep, every sound, and listening for any reassurance that her mother was alive. l hoped that she'd hear the sound of rescuers. I felt for her. She looked to be in absolute agony. She had to be, she was listening to the moments preceding the inevitable murder of her own mother.

As I heard the sounds of their voices, I knew Mrs. Maxwell was trying to beg for her life. She was using reason to try and convince the unreasonable. I didn't think she stood much of a chance. I just couldn't think of how this could possibly get any worse. We are sitting here hiding as we are about to hear a killing take place, and then we have to remain perfectly silent and hope and pray that a crazed lunatic then won't search the room. Those girls were going to give us away; I just knew it.

I thought about my own parents. They were so proud of me. I am their only child, their pride and joy. I wondered if they were waiting outside, yearning for me to bolt out of the doors and be safe in their arms. If they only knew, I couldn't be in a worse position.

I began to think about my father and all of the lessons he had tried to impart on me. "Aseem," he would say, "you must stand for justice in this world. We have been set apart so others look to us to do what is right." His words fell upon me like an order almost. I thought about him again. He was so proud of being a Sikh. When I was younger, I hated that I stood out, but as I'd gotten older, I hated it a little less. My father told me we were called to do great things. This stuck me as almost ironic that I, a kid who was currently hiding in a cabinet, could be the doer of great things. But, my father had believed in me. He told me that he had had a premonition about me once. His vision came to him in a dream where I was prisoner, and suffered greatly, but in the end, I used a clever trick to free myself of the chains around me. I then freed the other prisoners and we became victorious over our captors. Sadly, my father would likely never see me as heroic or even cunning.

Just then, I heard the sounds of an all-out physical fight within the room. I looked at the counselor's daughter, and her eyes were wide, and her face look determined. I could tell she had begun contemplating doing something. My legs felt weak. Were we about to hear the screams of her mother?

I thought about Mrs. Maxwell for a moment and how we'd met. She had always showed kindness toward me and a genuine interest. I hated to think of her suffering. I remembered how she compassionately asked me about being a Sikh. It blew my mind that she'd asked me about the 5 'K's'. I thought back about that conversation and how I had ended up lying to her. My parents had warned me against taking the Kirpan to school because being caught with a dagger could have meant immediate expulsion. I think a blade of three inches meant you were getting kicked out no questions asked. In rare rebellion, I had decided to wear it under my clothes anyway. I knew I would have to lie if anyone ever asked, but to be honest, I thought no one would ever take the time to do the research.

And, then it struck me. I had a weapon. I had a weapon on me that could possibly save her. I reached into my waistband and felt the metal blade. I didn't know if I could really do it. But,

I pulled the dagger out to hold it in my hand. At the least, I would use it if the cabinet doors were opened by the shooter. I caressed the handle of the dagger in my hand as I considered what to do. I weighed my options. I could stay safe or safer at least by remaining silent or I could make my family proud by defending the defenseless. I just didn't know if I could do it, though. My hands began shaking uncontrollably. Why was my body fighting against me too? Should I take the bold step or pray to remain unnoticed?

Chapter Twenty-Five—Cassidy

Mom had once again tucked me away for safe keeping. I had my ear pressed to the door and I could hear Mom's voice followed by a male voice. I thought optimistically for a moment that perhaps it was a rescuer. But, I quickly knew that wasn't the case. Mom's tone sounded desperate. I could tell she was pleading, coaxing, and finally begging for her own life, and in turn, our lives, too. This had to be the worst kind of pain that could ever be inflicted on a person. Thinking of the person you love more than anything being threatened, and feeling beyond helpless.

I thought about the instructions Mom had given me. She had told me to stay put, no matter what I heard. I knew this is what she meant. She meant that I'd have to stand by and hear her being executed. Anger rose up in my chest and filled me up. I listened harder and I could hear the shooter clearly say, "Don't move." This was it, wasn't it? He was going to take a shot. I braced myself, but then, I heard movement, the legs of desks screeched across the linoleum floor. I could hear what sounded like a fight. Had Mom been able to get the gun?

It was a do or die moment. I could obey Mom, the rule follower that I was, or I could break out of the cabinet and try to help her. On the one hand, Mom would surely die if I stood by and did nothing, but she wouldn't have to see me get shot. On the other hand, I could break our pact, and possibly save her, or the worst could happen, we could both get shot and I would expose the other kids, too. It was pure torture thinking about these two bad options. It wasn't like I even had a weapon, so was I kidding myself to think I could try and save her using my own brute force.

Just then, I glanced at Aseem. He would absolutely panic if he saw me make a move to open the cabinet. I looked down at his hands, and thought my hysteria had made me delusional for a minute. I thought I saw a knife in his hands. I eyed his hands again more closely, and I confirmed the impossible. I was actually in clear sight of a weapon, one that could be used to really fight back. Possibly fight back and win.

I gazed at Aseem right in the eyes, and looked down knowingly at his hands. He gave me a nod acknowledging that we were on the same page. His hands were shaking like a leaf. I looked at Aseem and gave an encouraging nod. I was confirming we were going to work together and risk it all without saying a word. He lightened his grip on the dagger and was able to gain control of his grip and his breathing. A steely stance came over him as he put his mouth to my ear and said, "for a noble cause." I nodded, and creaked open the cabinet door just slightly.

As I stared out the small crack, I could see Mom lying flat on her back with the shooter laying on top of her. She had fear in her eyes like I had never seen before. The shooter was just some kid. Some stupid, kid with a deadly weapon and a death wish. I leaned in to hear what was being said.

"Well, well, Mrs. Maxwell, you have put up quite the fight. I must say, I didn't know you had it in you," the shooter taunted her.

"Jason, please rethink this. I have children and a husband. You can't take away their mother," she pled as she tried to appeal to some sense of goodness in him.

In that moment, I made a decision. My mom wanted me to live, but living wasn't worth it if I couldn't live with myself afterwards. Aseem and I shared a final glance at each other and I lunged out of the cabinet, taking them both by surprise. I will never forget the look on Jason's face right before the dagger pierced his neck. He had become the prey and he looked every bit the terrified animal. Aseem stabbed the dagger deep into his neck and he reached for it with both hands. As his instinct took over and he tried to pull out the knife, I grabbed the gun and held it on him. Blood poured from his wound and he fell flat to the ground. Mom and I clasped onto each other so tight it was as if we would never separate again.

"Cassidy! Aseem! You saved me!" Mom exclaimed through tears of relief and joy. In that instant, our roles had suddenly reversed. Now, I was the caretaker and comforter. Tears rolled down our faces in a steady stream. The tears were a release of all the fear and tension we had experienced, and tears of indescribable, deep gratitude.

Aseem stared at us with dark, brown eyes. First, there was hesitation in his movement, and then a wide smile took over his face. He took another step toward us and joined us in an embrace. He was free of the paralyzing fear of staring his own mortality in the face, and had fulfilled the prophecy. I have never felt so grateful for another person in my life.

"Aseem," I said, "I owe you my life." And Aseem stared back at me with a gentle smile and a look of true peace.

Mom grabbed the walkie, and reported in. "The shooter has been disabled. We are in the Overflow Room." Within minutes, Mr. Bagwell showed up at the door and took charge of the scene. He first went over to Jason and checked his pulse. He still had one. But, he was unconscious from the loss of blood. Mr. Bagwell turned his head to the side and we could all see his face. He looked so young and helpless now with his eyes closed. Mr. Bagwell placed cuffs on his hands, and called for back-up.

"I'm going to need back-up, boys. And, we need a medic right away," Mr. Bagwell said very authoritatively. Mr. Bagwell looked at us with respect. "You all really kept your cool," he said as he nodded with admiration. "Weren't there others in here?" he asked.

"Oh, yes," Mom replied, "Check that cabinet." Mr. Bagwell opened the cabinet and he saw Ansley and Emily huddled together refusing to exit.

"It's OK, girls. You are safe. You can come out now," Mr. Bagwell reassured them. The two of them slowly stepped out. They looked around and their relief turned to shock as their eyes focused on Madison's body lying on the ground.

At that time, I handed the gun to Mr. Bagwell and ran to be with Madison. My worst fears were confirmed. It was too late. She wasn't breathing anymore.

"Mom," I cried, "she's gone." I crumpled onto the floor and sobbed in a heap. It felt surreal to lose her. I felt as if a part of me had died, too. Madison was the one person who really knew me. She was as close to me as a sister, having lived life with me right by my side. There was no other person besides my family, not even Trey, who I knew beyond a shadow of a doubt would never leave me. But, I was wrong. She did leave me, and there was nothing I could do about it. I felt heartsick and physically sick. Mom ran over to me and put an arm around me not saying a word. There were no words. She knew that there was no way to make this better.

Just then, the other members of the Safety Department arrived along with the emergency responders. They placed Jason on a stretcher and prepared to take him to the hospital. How was it fair that he was going to leave here alive and my Madison who was the best friend anyone could ever ask for was sacrificed?

Mr. Bagwell instructed us that he would have to clear out this room and barricade the entrance since it had become a crime scene and there was forensic evidence to be gathered. Police officers escorted us out of the school where it was like the whole town was waiting.

All of the other students had already been evacuated. Dad and Trey made their way to us. Trey picked me up and held me tightly. Dad hugged Mom and then grabbed me, too. We couldn't even speak. It was as if words were too small for the experience that we'd been through together.

I looked across the parking lot briefly and my eyes caught Aseem and his family embracing. I mouthed to him, "thank you." He smiled at me and nodded. Aseem and I would be bonded forever from this point forward. At first glance, Aseem and I couldn't be more different, but at our heart, we were the same. Just two kids trying to do the right thing, wanting to be heroic, doubting ourselves, and finally against all odds, proving that we were brave.

Chapter Twenty-Six—the Aftermath (Cassidy)

After the shooting and all the events that transpired, we knew we'd never be the same. We tried talking about it or processing it as Mom liked to say, but it would cause too much anxiety. I felt like Charlotte was oddly handling everything the worst. She was barely talking to anyone and wouldn't let Mom and Dad out of her sight. She was sleeping with them full-time again. It crushed me to think about her innocence being taken, and she now had to view the world through a jaded lens just like the rest of us. Mom said she'd be getting her into counseling soon.

Within a few days following the shooting, Madison's funeral was approaching. Her mother was a complete basket case. She was at a total loss without Madison. She asked me if I could possibly speak at the service since I knew Madison better than anyone. I didn't know if I could do it without breaking down, but I owed it to Madison to try. She deserved the best—the best in life and in death.

The night before the service, I stayed in my room trying to decide what to wear. I settled on a black dress and a black blazer with a pearl necklace and pearl earrings. I started working on what I was going to say. I took out my journal and turned to an empty page. I began thinking about some of my favorite moments with her and made a few notes. It was hard to limit my memories with Madison to the best ones. We'd been together through everything. I had thought Trey was my soulmate, and I still loved him like crazy, but if we're only given one soulmate in life, then it had to be Madison. I couldn't stand the thought of being without her, but I did feel beyond lucky to have had her when I did. I even still talked to her despite her physical absence—it was like she was still here with me. I would look up towards the ceiling and begin telling her what was going on. I didn't care if it was weird.

I looked up now, and asked, "Mads, what can I say about you? I think you'd want this to be real and not too stereotypical depressing. I hope I can do you justice." I started working again, even smiling some, as I remembered some of our funniest memories. I went to my laptop and started looking at some of the videos we had made in recent years. I pulled up the one that was dated a little over two years ago. Two goofy fourteen-year olds. Braces and all. In the video, we were singing a classic Whitney Houston song, "I Will Always Love You", at the top of our lungs and totally off-key. "And, IIIIIIIIIII will always love yoooou," we shrieked into the camera. We broke down laughing in the video and I noticed something I hadn't seen before. In the video, while I was rolling on the bed cackling, I saw Madison's face become serious. She said quietly, "Hope so." Oh, how this cut me to my core. Madison had the hardest time believing that love could last. I started crying. I looked up towards the sky again, and said aloud, "I always did and I always will."

The next morning, the time I had been dreading had come. We were to be at the funeral home at 10:00 AM. Trey came to our house to ride over with us at 9:00. I heard his car pull up and peered out of the window. I saw him get out of his car looking very somber. He was dressed in a dark, gray suit, with a white button down, and a navy and silver striped tie. He looked impossibly handsome, but I couldn't focus on that now. He made his way to the door. I opened up the door and immediately wrapped my arms around him and buried my head in his chest. He held me tight, and then leaned in to ask me how I was holding up.

"I'm not that good, Trey. I miss her so much," I said honestly.

"I know, believe me, I know," Trey said as he pulled me in closer again.

We got the rest of the family together and we piled into Dad's car. The ride over was very quiet. Mom asked me if I felt ready, and I told her I did. I wasn't sure, but I was ready as I was ever going to be.

We saw Madison's mom when we got there. And, she didn't look well at all. She looked frail, and was being propped up by her brother, Madison's Uncle Joe. She saw me and motioned for me to come closer. She pulled me in for a tight embrace.

"You were her everything, Cassidy. I hope you know that," she said.

"And, she was mine," I said.

"Thank you for speaking today. I knew there was no way I could stay composed and I knew Madison would want you to."

"I hope I make her proud, and you, too," I whispered. I gave her one last hug and walked into the chapel to find a seat. We sat near the front and I looked through my notes.

As 9:30, the chapel began filling up. People just kept pouring in. I think most of the school was coming to pay their respects. Inside, this made me beam with pride for my friend because I knew Madison would be pleased. The crowds just kept coming. Mr. Johnson, our Principal, arrived, along with Coach Brown, Mr. Holley, and the rest of Madison's teachers. The whole Front Office staff arrived together and were crying before they even found their seats. Madison had been their friend. They loved her working with them, and she had kept them thoroughly entertained. I only hoped Madison knew how many people she had touched.

Finally, the clock chimed ten times indicating that it was time for the service to begin. The pastor stood up and everyone rose as we sang the hymn, 'Be Not Afraid'. The pastor instructed us to be seated following the hymn, and began his sermon. I kept drifting in and out between listening to him and thinking of Madison.

"It is always hard to say goodbye to someone who dies suddenly and someone who had lived a short life in terms of years. However, it is true that a person's life cannot be measured in terms of length, but more so, in terms of depth. By the crowd I see here today, I know that Madison had lived a full life, touching so many. By all accounts, Madison was beautiful both physically and in her character. She brightened all of the rooms in which she entered, and left each of us, better off having known her," the pastor consoled us.

I began thinking of Madison again. I looked over my notes, and waited for the pastor to introduce me. I tried to gather every ounce of strength and poise I had. I prayed, "Dear God, please give me the right words, and the strength to relay them," and in that moment, I heard my name being spoken.

"And now, Madison's dearest friend, Cassidy Maxwell, will speak about Madison's time here on earth, and remind us all to treasure those moments we shared with her."

I stood, and walked to the front of the chapel with shaky knees and trembling hands. I cleared my throat and rested my note cards on the podium before me. Here goes, I thought.

"First, let me say, thank you for coming today to pay your respects to Madison and her family. I know she would be blown away by all of you. One thing about Madison, she loved to be loved. And, I get so much comfort knowing that she truly was adored by many.

Madison was my best friend since the age of four. She was my 'go to' person for everything. If something good happened to me, I called Madison right away. If I was upset or down, Madison was the first person I wanted to talk to. She always wanted the best for me, never jealous or envious, but my biggest supporter. I miss her more than I could ever express. There's something about a best friend—they are more than a friend, more like family, but the family you want to spend time with," I paused for a minute as laughter filled the room.

I started again, "People may think it's such a shame that Madison died before she had a chance to do anything great with her life. And, believe me, it is a shame that her life was cut short, an infuriating, enraging one, but not because Madison didn't get to do anything great with her life because she did. She got to be a great daughter, always looking out for her mother and helping to take care of everything at their home," I said as I looked over at Madison's mom still burying her face with a handkerchief. I continued, "she got to be a great friend, always there to listen, always ready for an adventure, and loyal to the end," I had to stop for a minute and take a deep breath, before finishing, "and Madison also got to be a great person, she was beautiful, but that wasn't the most important thing about her, she made people feel good, she really listened to people," this time I looked over at the Front Office ladies and they were nodding in agreement. I began again, "she made you feel cared about whether you were a friend's nine-year-old little sister," I looked over at Charlotte and winked, "or a Latin teacher, or a friend's mom," and I stared right at Mom and nearly lost it. "I will forever be changed for the good for having known her and I know I'm not alone," I ended as I stepped down from the altar.

The biggest sense of relief filled every cell of my body. I had done it. I had given her a real send-off without crumbling to a blubbering heap. I looked up towards the ceiling when I got back to my seat, and talked to Madison in my head, "So what did you think? I told you that you were a big deal."

Epilogue—Cassidy (Six Months Later)

Six months sure has changed a lot. Trey and I have now entered a long-distance relationship. I miss him so much, but we still get to see each other a lot. Everyone kind of got over the age difference and all that other stuff after the shooting. We have a bond tighter than most, and I can't see anything changing that.

School has been okay. At first, it was really hard to enter the school building. We've started to move on, but will never forget. I see Aseem almost every day. He's very well-known and is almost a celebrity at school. We always smile at each other when we pass one another. He is a good person and I'm glad everyone knows it now.

Mom and Dad are back in their routine. Mom has been asked to speak at schools all over the state. I think she's enjoying her new mission and spends time talking about the need to notice those that are overlooked. I'm proud of her. We really don't fight anymore because all the little things just don't seem that important anymore.

Charlotte is finally coming around. She still sleeps with Mom and Dad, but she's been going to a play therapist. Mom told me she acts out different things with figurines to express herself. Mom says most of the time she's the heroine in the story, and that is her way of trying to regain control. She's not as care-free as she used to be, but I catch glimpses of her silly self sometimes. Everyone says, "kids are so resilient", so let's hope that's true. I love that kid.

Madison is missed beyond belief. Her mother has really straightened up. She enrolled in an ultrasound technician program and is really focused. She says she is trying to make Madison proud. I know Madison has to know and is proud of her. We invite Madison's mom over about once a month, so we can keep in touch. She's struggling, but she's making it.

Jason, the shooter, survived his injury and is locked away. Apparently, he has some remorse about Madison. Some say that he was a victim, too. I can't forgive him, but I do think about what made him the way he was. Maybe one day I can forgive, but not now.

And me, I feel different. I'm not sheltered anymore, not over-protected, and not naïve. I miss my innocence sometimes, but there's no going back. I'm becoming stronger every day. I still talk to Madison and see her sometimes in my dreams. Strangely, I've begun to see more beautiful things in life—usually the little things that I'd never taken the time to notice.